Hello, My Name Is Henry

by: Micah Schnabel

Published by White Gorilla Press
Belford, NJ
www.whitegorillapress.com

Cover illustration, cover photo and interior illustrations by Vanessa Jean Speckman.

Cover and interior layout by Paulette Poullet.

Edited by Michael Baron and Paulette Poullet.

ISBN: 0-9884489-6-4
ISBN-13: 978-0-9884459-6-3

Hello, My Name Is Henry

Micah Schnabel

Chapter 1

Hello, my name is Henry. I'm 28 years old and I work in this gas station in Brooksville, Ohio. I'm the guy you ignore who's mopping the floor at two in the morning when you come in for your condoms or energy drinks or cigarettes. Or you're just passing through on your way to somewhere else, and when you whisper under your breath walking back to your car, "who in the hell lives in this place?" — The answer is me.

"Hey Henry."

"Hey Steve. How was your night?"

"The Halcourt kid came in and did 12 shots in an hour. I called him a cab and dumped him in. That kid's gonna kill somebody some day."

"I'm surprised he hasn't already."

"Reds?"

"Reds."

"How's business, Steve?"

"The younger crowd wants to drink and fight and the old timers want to drink until they fall asleep. They want the music that was popular when they were in high school and a pool table to kill the time in between fights. But it pays the bills. "

"That sounds terrible."

"It is and it isn't. It's a living."

Steve owns the Angry Steer, one of the bars downtown. The Angry Steer caters to the all-day drinkers and your general hard luck stories. It has two TVs above the bar that always have some sort of sporting event showing and even though there was a smoking ban passed 10 years ago, you can still smoke inside. It's understood that the green beer cans are actually ashtrays. It closes at 2:30 AM but opens right back up at 6:30 AM for the third shifters to come in and finish their day with a couple of drinks and easy bar conversation. And no matter what time of day it is outside it was always dark inside.

Steve comes into the store every night after closing to get cigarettes. He'd fill me in on all of the gossip and fights. And with the town being so small, I always knew at least one of the main characters in the story. I didn't want anything to do with the drama, but I did enjoy the stories. Especially at three in the morning, looking at four more hours left in shift.

“I thought Halcourt was in jail?”

“He was. He just did nine days for not paying child support. Just got out today. I should’ve stopped serving him after the first six shots, but I try to stay on his good side. And I figured if I got him drunk enough I could keep him under control.”

“Kill him with kindness, I guess.”

“He kept showing me his new tattoo he got while he was in jail. ‘Fuck the world’ underneath his right eye. The guy is terrifying.”

“Geezus.”

“Right? What do ya do with shit like that? You here all night?”

“You know it.”

“Alright, stay safe in here, Henry.”

I'd been hired to cover the night shift three years ago when the last guy quit after being robbed. That was the game of the night shift. How much were you willing to put up with, where was your line? Night-shift workers in a convenience store don't usually last long. They either work their way up to day shift or quit when they get tired of unplugging the tampons from the toilets, cleaning the bathrooms of the used needles and condoms and other things you wouldn't believe even if I told you. Or you get robbed and decide it's not worth your life for the extra dollar an hour you get for working the hours no one else wants.

After my first six months I got offered to move to the day shift, but by then I had decided I didn't mind working nights. Once you got used to it you could get into a rhythm of almost dodging life entirely. Which, at that point in my life, was exactly what I was looking for.

There was a short rush after the bars closed on the weekends but after that, things got pretty quiet. Every once in a while, someone would come in and demand change, saying the payphone out front didn't work. There were always a couple of junkies or drunks here and there and the occasional senior citizen who existed solely on nicotine and lottery tickets. They knew it was four in the morning, but they hadn't had any reason to regulate their sleep schedule for so long that the time on a clock meant nothing to them anymore. And a walk to the gas station was a reason to leave the house or apartment for a few minutes. And I understood that completely.

Chapter 2

7 AM

"Morning Henry."

"Good morning, Mel."

Mel is the usual morning clerk and the person who's been here the longest. She gets first dibs on any extra hours and first choice of days off. She comes in at 7 AM and takes over just as the school teachers and the few blue collars shuffle through the door to perform their morning rituals. Forty-eight ounce thermoses of coffee and 14 packages of Sweet'n Low stuffed into their pockets and one secret cigarette out front next to the ice bin before their day begins.

She was born when Jimmy Carter was president, but she looks like she was born under the Lyndon B. Johnson administration. No dental insurance and eating from gas stations and fast food joints every day, it takes a toll. When your entire life is trying to figure out how you're going to feed yourself and your family that day or how you're going to come up with three-hundred bucks to fix the car to get the kids to school while you're working 36 hours a week at a gas station making nine dollars an hour before taxes. It ages you.

"How was the shift? Any trouble?"

"Someone threw up all over the men's room. By the looks of it, I doubt they made it home. My guess is they are dead in a gutter as we speak."

"If only I were so lucky."

"Not a good morning, Mel?"

"Don't have kids, Henry. That bathroom is what my place looks and smells like every day. No matter what I do. Maybe I'm just tired. Don't listen to me. Fuck your own life up, you'll figure it out."

This is how Mel spoke. Every morning a new tragedy.

"The littlest fucker bit me this morning when I was trying to get him dressed. Kids these days have no respect for adults. Not like we did when I was a kid. If I would have tried anything like that my parents would have knocked the shit out of me. No questions asked. But now we're not supposed to hit 'em. How are they gonna learn if I'm not allowed to teach them? And all because I was trying to get him dressed for school. Ungrateful little shit."

"Where'd he bite you?"

“Right here on my arm. Look at this shit.”

She extends her right arm towards me and sure enough, there’s a small human’s dental x-ray still pressed into the flesh. A laugh jumps out of my mouth that I immediately regret.

“You think that shit is funny?”

She says it in anger and my heart skips a beat. I don’t breathe again until she looks at her arm and starts to laugh herself.

“I had both of his arms in his shirt and he wouldn’t put his head through the damn head hole. He’s wiggling around and fighting me every inch of the way. So I reach up and under into his shirt to try and pull it down over his head and he bites me!”

As she’s describing the situation she starts laughing even harder. Each laugh causing the other person to laugh harder.

“And it was a goddamned button-up shirt!,” she says, laughing so hard now that she’s using her own shirt to wipe tears from her eyes.

We’ve almost caught our breath when the doorbell dings and we both pull it together.

“I’m all counted out, Mel. You need anything before I go?”

“A million bucks and a Xanax. But nothing you got, Henry.”

Chapter 3

My mother was 17 years old when she had me. It wasn't unusual for a 17 year-old girl to come up pregnant in Brooksville, so aside from a few whispers and laughs from people, things went along as normal.

Her father, my grandfather, was a terrible human being. He believed the world had missed out on him and all of his brilliant ideas. He believed there to be some kind of unrecognized greatness inside of him that had never been appreciated. Some untapped brilliance he was just waiting to unleash on the world. And maybe there was. But the reason it was never found was no one's fault but his own.

The feeling of never reaching his potential or expectation of himself grew and exposed itself in dark and terrifying ways. He made a habit of cleaning his gun while having "talks" with his wife and daughter. He drank away every cent he and my grandmother ever made and blamed their desperate financial situation on people who had different color skin than his.

Whenever we spent any amount of time around the man my mother would spend the next two hours explaining away everything he had just said to me. Words I didn't yet understand. Words we have all heard. I don't feel right repeating them, so I won't. No matter how small of a role he played, he made it very clear to me in my limited time with him that we were "blood." That the same blood he had was running through my body. He once screamed this at me while my mother pulled me by my arm out of the front door of their house.

My mother had asked to hear one of his big ideas. She was trying to be encouraging, but he was drunk and took it as sarcasm. He made some vague, what I now know to be, anti-Semitic slurs while murmuring about a bank loan and then called her an uppity bitch and a whore for not believing in him and retreated back to his "office," which was the screened-in porch on the back of the house where he sat and smoked Basic 100 cigarettes and yelled about the government and drank Black Velvet whiskey and Coke out of glass jam jars until he passed out.

Truth is he had a hit in his early days after he left the military. A plan for a donut shop finally came into fruition after he talked himself into a bank loan, leaning hard on his military service. He had never seen any combat, but he did manage to cut the tip of his thumb off while peeling potatoes. I don't believe he mentioned that when he showed up to the bank with his honorable discharge papers in his hand and wearing a tie that his wife had tied for him because he couldn't get his hands to stop shaking from the booze withdrawal.

At that point in time, Brooksville and its people were still flush with manufacturing cash. The factories were running 24 hours a day and anyone who had graduated the eighth grade had guaranteed work that would pay a mortgage, a couple car loans, and leave enough leftover to take the family out to dinner. The movie theater had a line on the weekends and there were two bowling alleys cashing in on the last days of the modern-era attention span.

The donut shop was an instant hit. There were lines out the door every morning and the kids filled the place in the evening. It was my mother working the cash register and my grandmother in the back making the donuts. My grandfather walking around talking excitedly to himself and to anyone who would listen about how brilliant he was. Things were good for a moment and the money was rolling in.

My grandmother ran the place into the black, but even in this small-scale situation, trickle-down economics still didn't work. The profits never made it into anyone else's hands but my grandfather's. He spent the money faster than the donuts could fry and crashed his new car that he wouldn't let my mother or grandmother ride in into a telephone pole. When the bank and the landlord came calling and told my grandmother that neither the shop's rent nor the bank loan had been paid in two months she was dumbfounded.

She knew how much money had been coming in. Paying the rent on the shop and the monthly loan shouldn't have been a problem. But when she asked my grandfather where the money was he punched her in the mouth and told her how unthankful and unappreciative she was. Telling her how she should be thankful that she had such a brilliant husband and that he was tired of donuts anyway. He was ready to move onto something bigger and better.

My mother and grandmother didn't see him for two weeks after that. My grandmother was left to deal with the bank and the closing of the shop. Selling off the equipment to pay the back rent and try to catch up on the bank loan.

When my grandfather returned home two weeks later, bright-eyed and sharp in a new suit, he claimed to have a brilliant idea for a new restaurant that would finally bring them their fortune. My grandmother stayed quiet and my mother was left to bear the brunt of her father's mood swings. The new restaurant never came to fruition. There wasn't a bank in town that would even meet with my grandfather after the donut debacle.

The early donut-shop days seem to have been the last real good days of my mother and grandmother's lives. At least as far as I know. Any positive memory or story begins and ends with the donut shop. Occasionally my mom lets little bits of truth from her childhood slip out, but she never expounds upon them. After she brings them up she gets quiet and changes the subject.

Chapter 4

"Put the gun away, Ricky."

"Fuck you, Henry. Give me the fucking money and I won't shoot you in your face, ok?"

This is the third time that Ricky Stump has come in the store to rob me over the last two years. He comes in and waves his dad's old handgun around and tells me he's gonna shoot me until another customer walks in or I start to call the cops. He's twitchy and looking everywhere except at me. There's a jerky way of moving that only an addict can do. Eyes darting everywhere except where their focus should be.

He got into crushing Oxycontin and snorting it in his bedroom at his mom's house in his early twenties. His mom was in a minor car accident and had a prescription that the doctor kept refilling, no questions asked. It stayed recreational for the both of them until the pharmaceutical companies jacked the price up and the doctors started to get jumpy about putting their names on new prescriptions or refilling old ones. Ricky and his mother suddenly found themselves detoxing on weekday afternoons. It was a puddle jump from there to sticking needles in their bodies. He told me all of this himself when he used to come and hang out at the store and talk at me at four in the morning. Scratching lottery tickets and drinking

Mountain Dew the entire time and telling me how he couldn't sleep. This was back when he was still fighting the reality that he was an addict.

The doctors around here had been handing out painkillers for the broken backs of farmers and factory workers for years. Xanax Thursday was popular when I was in high school. Everyone's parents had a prescription of some kind hanging out in their medicine cabinet. Muscle relaxers and painkillers. Your grandparent's fentanyl patches you could stick on your leg before heading off to school. But the kids now have evolved and moved on. Xanax gets laughed out of the high school auditoriums now.

"Give me thirty bucks and I'll leave you alone. Come on, Henry."

"You know I can't do that, Ricky. I'd get fired for coming up short on the morning count."

"Just tell them you got robbed. It's not your money. Why do you give a shit?"

"I don't give a shit. But I'm telling you to fuck off with that gun. And if you shoot me, you're gonna have to spend the night detoxing in county. So just leave before I call the cops."

"Don't call the fucking cops. Just give me twenty bucks and I'll leave.

"Buy something or leave. You know there are cameras all over the place, right?"

Have you ever heard a gunshot up close? I hadn't until that moment. It was like my left ear drum exploded. Then a constant ringing in my left ear. I guess I was kind of in shock: First, that he had actually pulled the trigger and second, that he was just as surprised as I was. I think it was a moment of realization for him. The look of a person finally facing the lengths they would go to for something they wanted or needed, how little control they really had. It was a new level of desperation that neither of us had experienced before that moment.

"Shit. I'm sorry, Henry. It just kind of went off. Are you ok?"

"Did you really just try and shoot me?"

"No man! The thing just went off. I didn't think it even worked. I never even checked to see if it was loaded."

"I have to call the cops now."

"I'm really sorry, Henry."

Ricky's chin went to his chest like a sad child, like he was ashamed of himself. He covered his face with his hands and his shoulders started to heave. He was crying and sniffling and I really started to feel bad for him. I told him once more to leave.

"I'm sorry," he said again. It came out all muffled from his face being covered. He turned and headed out the front door.

I picked up the phone and dialed 9-1-1 and switched the receiver to my right ear so I could hear the operator.

"Yeah, 1311 Main Street. Someone just fired a gun in here .... I'm ok. I'm ok. But there's a hole in the wall .... No. I have no idea who it was .... I've never seen him before .... Yeah, I'll need to a fill out a report for my boss .... Thank you, ma'am .... I'll be here."

I hung up the phone and my body was buzzing. My heart was beating so hard I could feel it in my lips. I picked up one of the packs of cigarettes that were now scattered all over the floor behind me. I grabbed a book of matches and went outside and sat on the curb. I hadn't smoked a cigarette since I was 12 and stole one from my mom's pack on Thanksgiving. Back then, it had felt terrible and tasted awful. Like my lungs were going to cave in. But tonight, sitting on the curb outside of the front doors after having a gun go off in my face and a bullet whizz by my head, it was the most perfect thing I had ever tasted in my life.

I drew the first hit deep into my lungs just as the milk delivery truck rolled into the parking lot.

I heard a faint siren off in the distance.

Chapter 5

Henry,

Hey man! I haven't heard from you in a while and wanted to check in. I hope everything's okay in town. Sorry I haven't made it back in a while. I got a job at this pizza place down here and I'm trying to save up some money, so my weekends are pretty busy. I hope you're doing alright. Let me know when you think you can make it down and I'll take a couple days off work and show you around the city. Have you read the newest Memory Currency*?! You're still the only person I can talk about it with and I'm dying to talk about it!*

Your friend,

Josh

Josh,

It's great to hear from you! I'm trying to save up a little money to come and visit and hope to see you soon. I heard my first gunshot the other night at a rather close proximity and I can't wait to tell you more about it.

I figured out a way to have Memory Currency delivered to the store through one of the catalog distributors so that I can stay on top of the latest. I'm still getting through the newest one. They seem to have abandoned any kind of plot line. Robot Steve is working on a spaceship and Human Carol is working at some kind of space diner? I don't know where they're going with it but I'm too invested to get out at this point.

Your friend,

Henry

Chapter 6

Josh is my best friend. He has been since we both walked into elementary school dressed in hand-me-downs that smelled like stale cigarettes. We connected over the fact that nobody else in the school wanted us anywhere near them. What choice did we have? We could bond together or suffer alone. Misery loves company.

Kids in small towns with no athletic ability are left with very few options in recreational activity. We spent our time playing board games purchased secondhand at garage and yard sales that never had all of the pieces, forcing us to make up new rules as we went along. Think Monopoly with no dice and half of the money. Twister without the spinner and the mat reeks of cat piss. We came across what we now know to be a poorly written comic book called *Memory Currency* at a garage sale one afternoon while wandering through one of the nicer neighborhoods in town. We paid a dollar for a box containing the entire first series. It wasn't any good, and I think we knew it even then, but it was ours. All twelve of them. We forced ourselves to fall in love with it and we both continued to buy and read every new issue that came out over the years. I'm still not sure who the main character is or what the premise even is. Sometimes they're in space and then on the next page they're back on earth. There are no heroes or villains. It's a mess, but it's our mess.

Bonds forged at such a young age out of desperation tend to stick. High school was a war and Josh and I tiptoed around the landmines and smoldering bodies together. We were both the first in our families to graduate from high school. And while that seemed like quite a feat at the time, it turns out it's only a big deal to a certain class of the populace here in America. We were not aware of that while we were struggling to keep our heads above water in Algebra One in our senior year.

After graduation we decided to give ourselves one year to save money and prepare to leave. But halfway through the year Josh disappeared. I didn't hear from him for almost a year when one day a letter from him showed up in the mail explaining that he had left without me. It broke my heart but I understood.

Sometimes even when you really care for someone you can't keep yourself chained to them just to keep them comfortable. It only ends up hurting the both of you in the end.

Chapter 7

When you are living in a dying environment you can start to feel yourself dying with it. You're surrounded by people that have nothing and have grown bitter, so you start to become bitter. You become more isolated by the day. Every morning you wake up further from escape than you were when you went to sleep the night before. Even deeper in the hole.

The politicians are on TV telling us that immigrants are to blame, that they are taking all the jobs, but white people make up 96% of the population here in Brooksville. It's a trick, a sleight of hand, and no one seems to notice. Otherwise good people will do some awful things when they get desperate. It's like trapping a rat in a corner and being surprised when it bites you. And the people of Brooksville are the rat. Brooksville and all of the towns like it are the corner. All of us here are trapped.

And in their desperation, the people here keep voting for politicians that barely know they exist. It never fails. Some old white guy in a blue suit gets on TV and blames people of different races or nationalities or a religion for why you can't pay your mortgage this month and everyone jumps on board because it's always easier to think it's not your fault. That someone else is responsible for your problems. This tactic has been used since the beginning of politics. Put the blame for society's ills on a different skin color, religion, gender, nationality, and you've got yourself a voting bloc that will kill for you and your stale bread crumb of an idea that their unhappiness is someone else's fault. Never catching on to the fact that the person selling them these ideas is really the one to blame. A white male in a $10,000 suit telling us that if we were to make $15 an hour it would destroy the economy.

People still romanticize small-town charm. The little downtown square with a war memorial and a fountain. The main street lined with mom-and-pop shops. Charm is not a word that comes to mind while walking through the reality of downtown Brooksville. But people still hold these false ideas in their heads decades after the death of the dream.

Chapter 8

"Henry!"

"Hey Mom, how are you?"

"I'm good, Henry. Happy to see you."

Every job my mother has ever worked has been in the service industry. She's been moving from restaurant to bar to restaurant ever since I can remember. Wherever we happened to be living always smelled like a grease trap. The human brain is an amazing thing. The connections it can make when you're not paying attention. To this day a fast food cheeseburger is the taste of my mother's love. It means I'm safe and that there's enough money for fast food, instead of off-brand bologna on ValuTime white bread.

"Just have a seat anywhere and I'll bring you a menu."

"I'll just have a milkshake."

"Are you sure? It's on the house."

"I'm sure. I was out for a walk and thought I would stop in and say hi. How have things been?"

"It's been slow around here so money is tight as usual. But I'm ok."

"I wish you'd let me get you something to eat. They pay me $2.35 an hour here, plus tips. But it's really nothing but old folks coming in here, tipping whatever change is left over. I'm lucky to make seven bucks an hour on a good day. At least let me take advantage of the free meal every once and awhile. I can't eat this stuff anymore."

"$2.35 an hour? Is that legal?"

"I don't know. I'm happy to have the work so I try to not to fuss too much. No one else in town is hiring so it's kind of this or nothing."

"Sounds pretty close to nothing already."

"It is. But what else am I going to do? Anyway, how are you doing?"

"I'm ok. Ricky Stump came into the store the other night asking for money and shot a hole in the cigarette case. I'm still having trouble hearing out of my left ear."

"Are you kidding me? Are you ok?"

"I'm fine aside from the hearing. I have this high-pitched, faraway ringing thing happening, but it seems like it's starting to fade."

"That boy's crazy just like his father. It amazes me watching these kids. Like a videotape that just keeps replaying itself. The same mistakes over and over and over. Sit tight, I'll go grab that milkshake. I'm glad you're ok, Henry."

Pearl's Bar and Grill has been open less than a year, but there have been different restaurants in this building my entire life. People save up a couple bucks thinking their mother's cherry pie recipe is going to set the town on fire. They start with just enough money to get the doors open and aren't prepared for the first year in a new business, which is almost impossible to survive even if you have deep pockets, and as soon as the second month's rent comes due and it turns out that your mother's cherry pie recipe was just Betty Crocker's recipe written in your mother's handwriting on an old piece of paper, it's too late. And all of those late-night dreams of owning your own business and being your own boss and the eight years it took to save up the money to convince the bank to give you the loan is all gone. You file bankruptcy or sell the house. Or both.

This is why none of the tables and chairs match. The decor is a mishmash of sports memorabilia, pop culture, country home, and nonsense. The entire place is pieced together from our neighbors' broken dreams. My table is covered in old black and white photos of local high school football teams of the past, while the one next to me has a "Home Is Where The Heart Is" tablecloth with hearts and covered wagons. The rural poor love covered wagons for some reason. I have no theory or idea why. There's a framed Scarface poster on the wall back by the swinging door that opens into the kitchen. Poor people from everywhere love Scarface. I have many theories as to why.

"Here you are, Henry."

"Thanks, Mom."

"So what's up for the rest of your day?"

"I work tonight. I'm just killing time until then. I wanted to talk to you about something though, if you're ok to talk right now?"

"Hold that thought. I just have to run over and get Mrs. Henderson's drink order and I'll be right back."

"Don't worry about it, it's nothing important. I should get going anyway."

"Well, ok. If you say so. Thanks for stopping by, Henry. It's always good to see you. Come by the house soon and we can really sit down and catch up."

I stand up and lay a five-dollar bill on the table. I watch my mother rush on her tired legs over to her next table. White orthopedic shoes on a woman not even in her 50s. A body broken by poverty and bad habits.

For two dollars and thirty-five cents an hour.

Chapter 9

"Henry, don't wear that shirt to school tomorrow. The kids are going to make fun of you for the next three weeks."

This is the kind of advice I would have appreciated from my mom. Or anyone. Just a few little things here and there to help the days of adolescence pass a little easier.

My mom was always getting ready for work or already at work or still sleeping because she had worked late when I was getting ready for school, so even when I was really young, there was no one looking out for me in the wardrobe department. I had two pairs of jeans, there was a basket of me and mom's socks and underwear all tossed in together, and a hamper of t-shirts left over from summer sports teams and promotional giveaways from wherever my she happened to be working at the time. I was sent home from school twice for wearing, unbeknownst to me, t-shirts with alcohol advertisements on them. In the 90s, cigarette companies were using t-shirt cannons to provide clothing to poverty-struck youth all over the Midwest. These, for some reason, were within the small county school's dress code.

Jimmy Williams calls me the Marlboro Man to this day whenever he comes into the store.

Small things like how you dress can seem innocuous and superficial when you're young, but as you get older and realize you have not even the slightest idea of how to dress for a job that might pay more than $9 an hour, you can see how early on people can get left behind.

It's 4 AM and I'm thinking about all of this as I scrape yesterday's muck from the roller grill. I'm getting ready to put the sausage-and-egg breakfast sandwiches on when the bell dings, letting me know a customer has just walked in.

"Hey, Gina."

"I need cigarettes."

"What kind?"

"The cheapest ones you've got. Unless you feel like being nice to me."

"Nothing I can do about that, Gina. They watch these things like they're gold bars."

This town is a lot like prison in this aspect. Cigarettes are still smoked and widely accepted as currency. The word has gotten out that they kill you, but when you're looking down the barrel of spending your entire life making roller bearings or wandering around looking for things to put into your bloodstream to make you forget, the little warnings on the box don't seem so bad. New ideas and belief systems in America work their ways in from the coasts. They start in New York and Los Angeles and creep slowly through the cornfields. But even in this day and age of instant information it takes a long time for the big ideas to take hold this far into the Midwest. My guess is cigarette sales still have a strong seven years left here in middle America. Followed by another five to ten of slowly declining sales.

"Just the lights then. We go to school together?"

"For like 12 years, Gina."

"Huh. Time flies, I guess. You have a girlfriend?"

"Not at the moment."

"Right. You know, I remember you now, Henry. I always thought you were a faggot. Little faggot Henry."

"That's a stupid word."

"What the fuck did you just say to me, Faggot?"

"That's a stupid word. You're just repeating bullshit you hear from your friends."

"Fuck you, Faggot. Little faggot Henry. Come on, Henry. Come over here and prove to me you aren't queer."

"That's $4.96 all together."

"Come on, Henry. Come show me you ain't no fag."

"Please just pay and go, Gina."

"Kiss me, Henry. You faggot!!"

“What’s with all of the bite marks all over your arms, Gina?”

It happened in a flash. My left eye lit up with heat and I could feel the little sparks of light shooting through my brain. I fell back towards the cigarette case and tried to stay on my feet with my hands covering my face. As malnutritioned and sunken as a heroin addict can be, she sure could throw a punch.

“Fuck you, Henry! And I’m taking the fucking smokes!”

The door bell dinged as she left and I steadied myself on my feet. I tried blinking a few times and everything seemed to be working. Painful, but not broken. The faint siren still ringing in my left ear from last week’s gunshot. All for an extra dollar an hour.

I headed towards the back to stick my head in the milk refrigerator case for a few minutes to help with the swelling.

It was 4:09 AM.

Chapter 10

“Good morning, Mel.”

“Nothing good about it, Henry.”

"For once, Mel, we agree."

"What in the hell happened to you? Looks like someone didn't like the cut of your jib."

"I don't know what that means, Mel."

"Your face! And don't play smart with me this morning. My day is shit and it's not even 7 AM. Come over here and let me look at it. Just like my kids. Always all fucked up ... That doesn't look too bad. Put some ice on it when you get home. What in the hell happened?"

"Unsatisfied customer."

"A customer did this? Do you know who it was? Did they take anything?"

"A pack of Basic Lights."

"No money?"

"It wasn't that kind of situation. "

"Did you say something stupid?"

"She did. I just called her on it and she didn't like it."

"No one likes that. Sometimes you just have to let stuff go. Especially with the customers. They're all piles of shit."

"She got to me. Some words just get under my skin more than others."

"She call ya a fag?"

"She did."

"Shit Henry, that ain't nothin'. Trust me. I've been called shit. That doesn't even rank on the scale of things I've been called. Just go home and put some ice on that eye. I'll mark the smokes up on the damaged sheet."

"Thanks Mel. You need anything before I go?"

"Nothing you can give me, kid."

It was a freezing cold January morning, but the cold air felt good on my eye. I pulled my jacket tight and cinched the hood, leaving just my eyes and mouth exposed. I put my hands in my pockets and remind myself to go through the lost-and-found to try and find some gloves tomorrow. I walk quickly down Main Street keeping my eyes on the sidewalk and trying not to destroy the icing and sprinkles on the donut in my pocket that I took from work. Hazard pay.

When I get home I open the door and the warmth from inside comes rushing out. I take my coat off and toss it on the floor before remembering the donut in my pocket. I reach in and try to slide it out without destroying the icing. The sprinkles are a lost cause. I slide it out carefully and am happy to see the icing held together pretty well. The thought of putting ice on my face makes me shudder. I go to the kitchen and get a glass of water from the faucet. I gulp it down. Then I turn the water on as hot as it can go and let it run over my freezing hands until it starts to burn. I walk into the bedroom and kick my still-frozen shoes off into the corner of the room and fall onto the futon mattress on the floor. The last thought that runs through my mind as I'm drifting off to sleep is that I left the donut out on the kitchen counter.

I fall asleep thinking of all of our wasted potential.

Chapter 11

"Good afternoon, Brooksville! You've got Randy Ranger here, bringing you the latest news and classic hits of yesteryear! Be careful out there this evening as the temperature drops down into the teens after sunset. I'll be back in two minutes and 12 seconds with today's birthdays and traffic report. But first, here's the 1958 hit "Lollipop" by the Chordettes!"

***

I wake up to my alarm clock at 3:30 in the afternoon and Randy Ranger giving me today's headlines in Brooksville. I turn the radio off and stumble into the kitchen to track down the donut I left on the kitchen counter. I hear a clank of metal from outside and look out the kitchen window to see the mail lady walking down the sidewalk and away from my apartment. I walk to the front door and open it up just enough to slide my upper body through and reach the mailbox without having to step on the freezing concrete of the front porch.

I flip through the mail and place the electric bill on the refrigerator with a red dinosaur magnet that was on the fridge when I moved in. I'm excited to see a new letter from Josh has arrived. I tear the envelope open, careful to not rip the letter inside. I stand in the kitchen barefoot and still in my clothes from last night's shift. Moving from foot to foot on the cold blue-and-white-checkered linoleum floor.

Henry,

Things are quiet here at work at the moment and Cher's "Believe" is playing on the radio and I just caught myself singing along and realized I needed some kind of distraction. I've been re-reading the latest Memory Currency *and I think Captain Jane may be a metaphor of some kind. I have no idea for what and I might just be reading way too much into the entire thing. Check it out and let me know asap. I hope you're well, my friend.*

Josh

***

I fold the letter back up and slide it back into the envelope. My feet have gotten used to the cold floor. I've stopped hopping from one foot to the other. I walk back to my bedroom and crawl back under the warm covers. I reach over and grab my copy of *Memory Currency* from the floor next to my futon mattress. Reaching past the Little Debbie snack wrappers and old water cups. I fall back asleep while searching for a deeper metaphor for Captain Jane.

Josh,

I'm reading through the latest Memory Currency now and I'm not finding any kind of metaphor anywhere. Especially with

Captain Jane. I understand that she took the Jetter Slide to some kind of new land and she seems to be the only human character in said new land. But they keep switching artists and making the whole thing even harder to follow.

And who keeps printing these things? Did you see the ad in the back for a jetpack? Looks like next week's paycheck is already spent. I'll keep digging through this and let you know what I find. It's always good hearing from you.

Henry

Chapter 12

Do you know where all those troops come from that people claim to support by putting bumper stickers on their cars? They come from little places like Brooksville. The military starts preying on these kids when they are 13 or 14 years old. The Navy, Army, Air Force, Marines, the whole bit. They show up in their clean-and-pressed uniforms and set up shop in the school cafeteria, right next to the glee club tables and prom committees. They stand there and smile and shake the hands of these kids that are still worried about acne breakouts and school dances. And they talk to them. The kids that have no real options. Both parents working in factories is a best-case scenario in these towns. You take a look at your last math test and the teacher is telling you you're a loser and you become convinced that you're not smart enough to handle the so-called real world all the adults have warned you about and all of a sudden you find yourself walking over to these tables to talk to these men and women with great smiles and perfect uniforms. It sounds a hell of a lot better than spending your adult life on a factory line making cars or boats or washing machines.

So it starts when you're a freshman in high school and over the next four years, they continue to show up. And with the word "hero" running through your mind, you fill out a little 3x5 index card that allows them to start calling you on the phone or emailing you after school. And they will call. And they will come to your house and meet your parents. They'll tell you about the opportunities that being in the service will create for you. And when you are young and naïve and invincible, it all starts to sound pretty good. My mother, in fact, was all for it. She said it would teach me discipline. Her father had been in the Army. He was very disciplined in the act of wrecking people's lives. He never took a day off.

They're here because they know exactly what they are doing. In these little towns you have all these kids that have nothing. And as far as they can see, they never will. I went to high school with a kid that had a dirt floor in the kitchen at home. This was in 1999. So when an opportunity like this presents itself to a kid like that, it looks pretty good. A steady paycheck and immediate respect from everyone and anyone you will ever meet. These are kids that have never had anyone show them any respect in their entire lives. Their parents call them assholes and their teachers call them idiots. And now they have a chance to be a hero.

I signed the notecard my senior year. I had no real idea what I was doing of course, but I did it. And I didn't tell anyone. But all I could think of was that the way people looked at me would change. No longer would I be invisible. I could be someone, a person that old people would stop and shake the hand of.

The recruiter is telling you what you want to hear, that you could be in the band or work with computers. That you'll likely never see a bit of combat, never be in harm's way. Just a steady paycheck, respect, and free travel. But I knew where kids like us went in the military. Kids like us went from boot camp to the front lines. We are the human fodder for all these causes and policies, all that bullshit. We're the expendable ones. The poor are always sent off to fight the wars the rich men pick. And the wars never end.

So when you hear about a tank full of soldiers getting blown up, those kids were people like me from places like this. How many 17- or 18-year old kids that you know are really all that patriotic? When you're that young you just aren't able to wrap your mind around what war actually is. You have no gauge for the actual violence and carnage that comes with it. Or the toll inflicting that kind of violence on another human being takes on the person inflicting it. Everyone loses.

When they had a ceremony on one of our last days of high school, I was blown away by how many people I knew had signed up. People with nowhere else to go, no one expecting anything from them. So they made the leap. But even then, with their recruiter who had promised them the world standing beside them and smiling, you could see the fear creeping into their faces. They had, with the ease of a signature and a handshake, become adults. I remember seeing them in the hallways after the ceremony and noticing how the teachers were speaking differently to them now. Respect. Finally. Everything the kid had ever wanted. Someone to talk to them like a human being. And all it took was sacrificing themselves to a war they had nothing to do with and didn't even believe in.

The biggest surprise of the whole bunch was my friend John. He was a smart kid. Unfocused, but smart. He even had some money. I mean, his parents did. Anyway, John signed up for the Army. And they sent him out.

When he came back from his first tour of duty, Josh and I went over to his house to see him. He had been drinking, but he seemed to be feeling alright. He was laughing and we talked. We didn't ask about the fighting. We tried to keep it light. But when the laughing and conversation slowed, John went back to his bedroom and when he came back he had a gun in his hand. I hated guns and John knew it. So he started waving it around and I tried to laugh and asked him to put it away. I get it, I said, big man with a gun now. And we all chuckled. I got up from the couch and started moving away from him. Just slowly, trying to play it all off like a joke. That's when he stopped laughing. He got real serious and started walking over to me holding the gun up in the air. I stopped laughing. I remember the look in his eye. It was like John wasn't there anymore. Someone else was behind the controls now.

I can recall every detail of that moment. Standing in that kitchen next to the front door with my hand on the counter and John pointing that gun in my face. He asked me if I was scared. I said I was. And then he smiled and pulled the trigger. I can still hear the sound of that click in my ears. I remember my next breath, and then John bursting into laughter. Saying he couldn't believe how scared I was. That he would never shoot me. I wanted to run out of there, but these were my friends. Josh tried to laugh it off for my sake, but I could tell he was just as scared as I was.

Same old Henry, John said. Still can't take a joke.

I guess so, I said.

John walked back to his bedroom, which I could see into from the kitchen. And I saw him pull his G.I. duffel bag out from underneath his bed. I watched as he unzipped it, popped a bullet from the chamber, and slid the gun back into the bag.

Chapter 13

A few years later John would use that very same gun to blow his brains out in the living room of his apartment right across the street from the Brooksville V.F.W.

He had just gotten home from his third tour of duty and was so scattered he didn't know which way was up. I had a really hard time with his death. It opened my eyes to a bigger picture of these little towns and the people inside of them. I didn't go to the funeral because the person that had died wasn't the person that I had known growing up. The kid in the KISS makeup in the Polaroid picture from a Halloween years back had died a long time ago. I didn't know that empty shell in that casket. I had no connection to it.

On the day of the funeral I remember Josh getting drunk and yelling about how we should go just to tell that smiley recruiter to go fuck himself. That sounded like a good idea but I would never have the nerve to go through with it. We both woke up in the morning feeling like shit.

Chapter 14

Laying here in this little room on my futon mattress on the floor with the lights off. My thoughts racing. They never stop long enough to allow me to focus. It's dark. And sometimes it feels like the darkness just makes the pictures come even faster. Made-up pictures of me and my father. The brain can be an amazing and terrifying thing. I can lay here and picture the death of everyone I've ever known. I can create images of my father and I standing on the fresh-cut grass in a front yard. Me in a little league uniform and him leaning down with his arm around me and we're both smiling. We look happy. But this never happened. My brain has made it all up. I have no idea what my father's face looks like. I guess probably a bit like mine. Just older.

If I lay here in the dark long enough I can almost convince myself that these things are real. But when I turn on the lights, I am immediately reminded of the loneliness that defines my existence. The room is empty. The only sound is from the cars rolling by outside.

Sometimes I hear kids walking by on the way to school. I like it when they are talking all excitedly. The way I used to. Or at least the way I think I used to.

Chapter 15

"WQRC! The Hits You Miss! Hello, Brooksville! You've got Randy Ranger here with you all afternoon. Bundle up out there today, folks, it's a cold one! We want to send a big WQRC Happy birthday out there to Wanda Johnson turning 52 years young today. You're not going to want to miss the Candle Light Gathering at the Bread Basket and Amish Offerings tonight at 7 PM. Make sure to dress warm! That's the news for now. We'll be right back after these words from our sponsors with the 1958 hit "Lollipop" by the Chordettes. Man alive, could those kids sing!"

***

It's 4 PM when I wake up for the day. Randy lets me know that I haven't missed anything in the world of Brooksville. I can smell my work clothes that I forgot to take off before going to sleep. It's a distinct combination of gas station meat, the stench of refrigeration, and cheap coffee. My eye feels a little swollen from getting punched last night, but it's a dull ache. I strip my clothes off, toss them in the corner, and head into the shower. As the warm water pours over me I search my brain for what day it is, only to come to the conclusion that it doesn't matter.

Chapter 16

There were lots of letters from Josh. Notes to remind me that there was more out in the world than just Brooksville. It may seem small, but these letters and notes are a big help to me getting through the day. I think Josh knows that, so no matter how busy he is, he always makes sure to keep them coming. I keep them in a stack in a drawer in the kitchen. Just small reminders of a world beyond my narrow existence.

Chapter 17

I don't have a car or even know how to drive so my options for travel are pretty limited. My grandmother owned a car for a while after my grandfather died, but she hated driving and never encouraged my mother to learn. As a result, Mom and I never had a car so I've always just existed in a small radius of wherever I happen to be living.

The only places I know to go during the day are the library, the grocery store, and the coffee shop that sits in the middle of downtown next to Brooksville's crown jewel, a small park at the main intersection with two benches facing a water fountain and a patriotic mural. In the summer people passing through town on their way to the lake will sometimes stop and look at the mural for a few minutes, but they quickly realize there's no further entertainment and they move the family another 40 minutes north on the interstate in search of something that isn't a chain fast-food restaurant or an unfortunately named locals-only diner.

Before I started working at the gas station I spent a lot of time at the library. I hated reading when I was growing up, but as I got older I started to find refuge in books. I really liked the idea of being smart even if I wasn't. At first I would check out books and carry them around with me, like a shield. I'd rarely get past the first chapter in most of them but I felt that if someone saw someone like me carrying books around they would assume I had something more going on. That I was more than just a kid with non-ironic holes in his pants wearing cigarette ad t-shirts two sizes too big for him. (Side note: Promotional t-shirts are almost always XL.)

Just carrying the books around made me feel a little better about myself. But as I got older I started making my way through the first chapters and even started finishing some of them, almost by accident. And as I started finishing them I could feel my shield getting stronger. Very few people are willing to disrupt someone deeply engrossed in a book. And for someone in my financial situation the fact that they were free certainly didn't hurt.

When I walk into the coffee shop I'm careful to not let the door slam. I try not to draw any kind of attention to myself. I'm the only person in here under 50. Older men and women are scattered around little wooden tables made by the Amish families out in the eastern part of the state and then trucked in to be sold as posh to the upper crust of these small rural towns. The Amish quietly do very well for themselves in rural America. They've rather ironically come into style.

I listen to fragments of some of the conversations as I wait to order and they all seem to be the same. Stories of the good old days or how the youth of today are ruining the country. Every generation thinks theirs was the hardest working and that the kids are lazy and if we could just get back to the fabled good old days. Problem is there were never any good old days. There's just a turning point where our emotional development stops. The world's situation was just as dire as it is now. As it's always been.

I have a theory that once a person stops reading, writing, listening to new music, experiencing new things, that person stops developing emotionally. They then find themselves in a stasis of sorts. That's when this *good old days* idea takes root. This is a large part of my fear about having stayed here so long. Have I already stopped developing? The very thought that I could someday look back on where I am now and be nostalgic is simply too much to think about. I ask for a small coffee. The lady behind the counter says nothing to me. She takes my money and quickly turns away. New faces are not welcome here.

The world keeps evolving and most of the people here dislike that very, very much. They vote down school levies for their own children and refuse any and all tax increases no matter what they are for. What's theirs is theirs and no one will take that from them. Not even their children. They starve out the youth and the town continues dying. This place and so many others like it have been dying a slow death for a long time. Unwilling to grow and change with the world surrounding them.

She sets my coffee on the counter without saying a word. I thank her. Silence. She again turns her back to me. Back to washing the single dish that sits in the sink behind her.

Sitting near the windows looking out onto the sidewalk and street are two older men. Both in overalls, wearing hats with seed company names on the front with mesh backs. They get together every weekday to bitch about the crops, who's died since they last talked, and the government. It's what their fathers and grandfathers did before them. Wake up too early. Complain about work. Bitch about the government. It never matters what the work is or what political party is in charge at the time. Whatever the circumstances, they are ready to bitch about them.

They had America in its heyday. They bought houses for twelve bucks and raised families on jobs they got right out of high school. And like every generation before them, they see the youth as lazy. They retell and retell their stories over and over again about how hard they worked to get to where they are. Even when the truth is it was all handed down to them. But they would never admit that. And since the world went ahead and changed while they were busy utilizing the privilege of not paying attention, they feel like somewhere along the line they were fooled and lied to. They both eye me suspiciously as I scan the room looking for a place to sit.

Two older ladies to my left are speaking in heated voices. I leave one table empty between me and them, I set my coffee on the table and sit down. I sit and stare out the window into the cold, grey Ohio afternoon. When you grow up in a cold environment, you learn to actually SEE the cold. It's the color of the circus not coming to town anytime soon. And if the clouds go away it gets even colder. I wrap my hands around the cup to feel the warmth. The words on the mug read: "God has a plan, and we have coffee!"

It never ends with these cutesy rural colloquialisms.

I unzip my jacket to let the warm air in. I slide my arms out one by one and let the jacket fall onto the back of my chair. I reach down into a jacket pocket and retrieve my small blue notebook with the pen inside of the coiled binding.

Dear Josh,

I got your letter today. I always appreciate hearing from you. I'm still trying to save up a little bit of money before leaving. I was going to ask my mom to borrow some but she doesn't have any either. Do you think I'd have a hard time finding a job down there? I want to make sure that once I leave I never have to come back.

It's really cold here today. That kind of cold that makes your hands sting and ache even after they've warmed up.

Ricky Stump came in the store last week and was trying to shake me down for the cash in the register. I told him to leave and he pulled the trigger and put a bullet in the cigarette case. It was the loudest thing I've ever heard.

As far as Memory Currency goes, I fear you may be in too deep. I'm currently investigating this Captain Jane situation and I'm just not seeing it. I'll let you know my thoughts in my next letter.

Henry

***

I set my pen down and pick up my copy of *Memory Currency* to investigate like I promised.

Chapter 18

"Excuse me, son. I'm sorry to interrupt you."

"Me?"

"Yes. I'm so sorry to interrupt you but we were just discussing some ideas here and since my dearest friend Kathleen seems to have lost her ever-loving mind, I was wondering if we might ask you for your opinion on a matter?"

"I'm not sure I can be of any help, but ok."

They launch right into it.

"It's a bit heavy, but I feel like we need a younger opinion .... Abortion is legal. It does not matter one bit if I agree with it or not. It should be available wherever it may be needed. Just the same as Kathleen's face over here. I don't agree with it, but it's a legal, medical procedure."

"Well Marjorie, if you wish to send your little old soul to hell than that is on you. Supporting these tramps. These kids out there having kids. It's evil. And supporting it, well, what does that say about you?"

"If I recall correctly, Kathleen, all three of your children were accidents. And how old were you when you had your first child? Nineteen, if I remember correctly. And you're going to sit here and give me this *kids having kids* nonsense. I remember the phone calls. Every single time. The crying, wondering what were you going to do. But you've forgotten all of that now? What it feels like to be scared out of your mind. Just a child in a terrifying situation no one has prepared you for. I suffered so let the children suffer? Have you really forgotten how scared you were? How you weren't even sure you even wanted children? Because I do remember."

"You know, Marjorie, I really think it would benefit you to come to church with Roger and I."

"Goddamn it, Kathleen. You've got to be kidding me with all this religious crap."

Marjorie turns to me.

"I'm sorry, what was your name, son?"

"Henry."

"Henry. You see how it is. We could really use a younger opinion."

"Umm. I'm sorry. I'm not really sure what to say."

"I understand. It's a bit heavy of a conversation to dive right into with strangers. But I'd honestly like to know your thoughts on the matter. Whether you agree with me or not."

"Well, I know how many Lightning Rods I sell every night."

"I'm afraid I don't know what that is."

"It's a pill, for guys. It's supposed to, you know, make them better .... I'm sorry ...."

"Sexually?," she interrupts.

"I guess so. At least that's what the package says."

"Such sensitive little boys. No offense, Henry."

"I sell about a dozen a night. To young and older people. If I can sell those to any 16-yearold boy that wanders in I don't see how you could tell a woman what to do with her body. My mom was only 17 when she had me. She still wishes she would've had another option."

"Ha! Lightning Rods. Where's your god now, Kathleen?"

"I'm tired, Marge. I should get going." The one called Kathleen stands up. She seems weary with it all, not angry, not really. "It was a pleasure, Henry .... I'll see you tomorrow at the house, Marjorie?"

"I'll be there."

The one named Marjorie gets up now and they hug one another.

Kathleen puts her coat on and bundles a scarf around her neck before heading out the front door. A rush of cold air comes rushing in when she opens it and hits her friend and I at the same time. We both wince.

The door shuts and closes off the cold air. Marjorie turns her body towards me in her chair.

"Thank you for the backup, Henry. She means well. I'm just trying to shake her out of this god phase she's going through. It's obnoxious."

"It was my pleasure. You were Marjorie?"

"Marjorie Wilkes. Pleasure to meet you, Henry."

"Nice to meet you, Marjorie."

"Please, call me Marge. Kathleen only calls me Marjorie when she's pissed off. She can be such a child sometimes. I think it comes from being the younger sibling. These little family identities never disappear."

"So you and Kathleen are ..."

"I'm older by two years. She's the youngest. Hence the bratty behavior."

"Only siblings can fight like that and still hug each other afterwards," I say, immediately worrying that I've said too much.

"Do you have any brothers or sisters?"

"Not that I know of. My mother only ever had me and I never met my dad. So as far as I know, I'm an only child."

"Sounds peaceful." Marge says.

"I think it would be nice to have someone that you could go back and forth with like that. Knowing everything would be ok in the end."

"Perhaps. It's hard for me to gauge at this point. So what brings you here today, Henry? No work today? No school? You're the only person here who wasn't alive when the wheel was invented."

"I work nights. I've been trying to wake up a little earlier to get some more daylight. The whole sun setting at 5 PM can be a bit of a downer for me."

"These Midwestern winters can be brutal on us sensitive types. Where are you working nights at?"

"The gas station on the south end."

"I see. If you don't mind me asking Henry, how old are you?"

"28."

"Not to pry. But kids don't stay here. There's not much here for them now. Not that there ever was, but there is even less now. What's keeping you here?"

"That's what I'm trying to figure out."

Chapter 19

A moment of silence passes between us. For once, I don't feel awkward in it. Marge begins to talk.

"I left when I was 18. I moved to New York City to become a dancer. Or a movie star. Or anything really."

"How did it go?" I ask. I'm worried about sounding too eager for the conversation, but she seems just as interested.

"Splendid. For a long time. I did a few commercials. Some waitressing and bartending, things to pay the bills. My parents complained that I was throwing my life away. That I was getting older and needed to think about the future and settling down. I was 23 years-old and they were telling me those things. A child! Settle down. That's what everybody wants for everyone. To settle down. Don't ruffle any feathers. "

"So you just went to New York City?"

"I did. And that was really something back then. For a girl to just up and leave on her own. But New York City was a different place back then. Someone like me could just go and find their way. I'm afraid it's not like that anymore. The grit's been swept away. Just another rich person's playground now. It's not the place that I fell in love with."

"So how long did you live there?"

"26 years. I came back here to visit when my dad got sick and I just never went back. I don't know why."

"It's hard to leave, isn't it?"

"It's scary. But not hard."

"People move to new places every day. But from here, the distance seems insurmountable. Some nights when I'm lying in bed and I get this fear that when I wake up I'm going to be 50 years old and everything will be exactly the same. Except I'll be older. I'm not talking about dream scary, I mean real-life fear."

"I know that fear. It happened to me. Or I allowed it to happen. I just came back one day and never left. It was just so easy to do, and that fact makes it so unrewarding. I miss waking up and knowing that I had to make 50 dollars to pay my rent. It was so terrifying sometimes, but looking back now, it was all part of the excitement. Every day held some new challenge and I had no idea what the answer was. And now here I am. Sitting here in this place arguing with my sister over whatever we choose to argue about that day. It's sad, really. But she never left this place. It's the only home she has ever known. I don't know. In the end, it doesn't really matter, I guess. We're sisters. Bound together, all the history, the blood. We would never choose to be friends out in the world. But we shared parents and that's a tough connection to shake."

"Were you ever married?"

"I never did get married. Or have kids. Ideas like that never really interested me. My parents were a mess. Always fighting. After I got away from them and that being my only model for relationships, none of it ever interested me. The house, the kids, the responsibility of it all."

"Go to work, come home, die."

"The thing is though we can choose to spend our time however we want, if we're brave enough. That's the trick. Politics, religion, school, acting, making music. All just different ways of killing our time. And none of it is really worth worrying about. Try and find something that brings you joy. To hell with the rest of it."

"That makes life sound easy."

"It is. If you let it be. It's all in how you look at it. It's just a game. Nothing more. What are you reading?"

"Oh, nothing. Just a comic book I read sometimes. I've read every single one they've ever put out and I still can't make any sense of it."

"The artwork looks nice."

"It is and it isn't. It looks like they changed artists after page 7 and the new one didn't pay any attention to what the old one was doing. The same characters, but drawn completely different. It kind of makes it hard to follow."

"Who's this?"

"That's Captain Jane. A friend of mine swears she's a metaphor for something but has no idea what. I'm trying to figure it out now."

"Well, enjoy yourself, Henry. It was a pleasure speaking with you.

Thank you for keeping this old woman company. I hope to run into you again soon."

She stood up and gathered her things and bundled into her winter coat. She tightened her scarf around her neck before pushing her way through the front door. A blast of January air whipped through the place scattering the notebook, pen, and my copy of *Memory Currency* onto the floor.

Chapter 20

I gather up my notebook and pen, the copy of *Memory Currency*. I put my coat back on and walk out the door, leading with my shoulder and keeping my head tucked away from the wind.

I think about what Marge said. About life being easier than we play it out in our heads. About all of the problems that we create for ourselves. Entire lifetimes lost to the anxiety of tomorrow.

I make my left to head towards home when I see Ricky Stump walking towards me. It's freezing outside and all he has on is a thin red sweatshirt with a football helmet on it.

Ricky stops. I stop. He shuffles back and forth on the sidewalk, moving back and forth on his toes.

"Hey Henry, what are you up to?"

"Just heading home. You?"

"Just hanging out," he says, eyes darting. "Hey man, I'm really sorry about the other day. I was freaking out a little and I didn't know what to do. And the gun going off, that's just fucked up. I'm really sorry. Thanks for not telling the cops it was me .... Fuck it's cold out here."

His eyes were everywhere. He couldn't stop himself from the constant jerky, unnatural movements. It made him hard to look at. I felt bad for both of us.

"Could you just not do that? Like .... ever again?"

I tried to say it loud to get his attention, but he didn't seem to notice. He kept looking in every direction except mine.

"Yeah, man. Of course. I don't know what I was thinking .... Hey, do you have a few bucks I can borrow? I'll pay you back. I'm just a little short right now."

I notice now that he's carrying a small plastic grocery bag filled with cans. This is the easiest way to make a desperate few quick bucks. If you can get to the dumpsters behind the bars before someone beats you to it you can make enough money to keep you good and forgetful for a couple days. The problem is beating everyone else to the loot. Addicts don't carry alarm clocks and the recycling trade is a real rat race nowadays here in Brooksville.

People make the mistake of thinking being an addict is easy. Just sit around and get forgetful. But that's the furthest thing from the truth. The chase is constant. Even if you have the thing you want you're already concerned about how you're going to get more tomorrow. There's no such thing as rest for an addict. That's one thing that my mom did teach me. The constant chase.

I read an interview in a magazine at work last week about this lady that works on Wall Street in New York City. She said she wakes up at 3 AM to study the other markets and do research before going into work at 7:30.She said she made 12 million dollars after taxes last year and she still gets up at 3 AM every day to go to work. I don't have any stones to throw at anyone trying to forget about life for a little bit. We wrap ourselves in warm blankets of money, heroin, loneliness, alcohol, exercise, business, busyness, whatever, it's all escape. And I get it. I don't see much difference between that lady and Ricky. The desperation for the next hit pushes us to do things we would never do if we were sane.

I pull my wallet out, hold out a five, and ask him to promise to never try and rob or shoot at me again. It feels like a reasonable investment. My own personal 401K. He tries to laugh it off, but I make him stop twitching for a moment and promise me. He does. Then he takes the five bucks.

"Thanks, Henry. I really appreciate it, man. I hate having to ask like this, but I'm just kind of in a spot right now. I'll pay ya back. I swear."

"Just don't try and rob me again. I don't feel like that's asking too much."

"Have you seen Gina today? Like, walking around or anything? We were hanging out last night, but when I woke up today she was gone."

"I haven't, man. Sorry."

"It's alright. I'll find her. She always pops up somewhere. If you see her will you let her know I'm looking for her?"

"Sure thing."

We stand like that on the sidewalk for a moment, pretending there is something else that we may have to say to one another. When nothing comes, I pull my hood tight around my head and start making my way home. I don't look back to see where Ricky goes.

Chapter 21

"Don't forget to move the cartons with today's date to the front, Henry. Milk waste has been way up this month. I can't afford to be throwing this stuff away. And make sure you're pricing every individual carton. And what in the hell happened in the men's bathroom?"

"I don't know, Mr. Clark. I'll check it out as soon as I get done over here."

I'm hunched down with half of my body inside of the milk cooler making sure the cartons that were marked to expire in the next couple days are all moved to the front. Holding the door open with my body and holding the pricing gun in my right hand. I've forgotten to put the gloves on and my hands are now bright red from being inside the cooler for the last 20 minutes. Mr. Clark stands a couple aisles over, near the front door, yelling to me over the racks of junk food.

"I'm sorry. I don't mean to be barking orders at ya. Six in the morning yelling about milk. You've been working all night."

The last part he says more to himself. Reminding himself of our current situation.

"I'll finish this up, Mel won't want to do it when she comes in." I yell over the racks. "And I'll hear about it, not you. No offense."

"None taken. Mel scares the hell out of me. My wife hired her five years ago and I don't have the guts to fire her." He pauses then continues. "What are you doing here, Henry? You're a bright kid. You could find something that pays a little better, at least."

"But who'd price the milk?," I say, trying to keep things light. No dice.

"The whole gunshot thing the other night. And then I saw that girl punch you in the eye the other night on the security camera. I was going through the gunshot footage to send it over to the cops. I couldn't really see the kid's face because of the angle. I knocked that camera crooked a year ago when I was trying to dust it with a broom and never got around to fixing it. They said there isn't much they can do. Anyway, are you doing ok? It's been a lot the last few weeks."

"She got me pretty good."

"It looked like it. What'd you say to her?"

"Nothing really. She was just angry. She was going to hit someone, I just happened to be in front of her at the time."

Mr. Clark is the owner of the store. I only see him once or twice a week. He comes in to check on things and get the money from the safe to drop off at the bank as soon as it opens. We usually engage in a little small talk and I don't feel uncomfortable when he's around. He used to be a teacher at the high school and though I was never a student of his, I never heard anyone complain about him either.

"The milk and candy aisles can find someone else to stock them. The last few overnight clerks I've had haven't been quite as," he pauses, carefully choosing his next word. "Reputable, maybe? If you catch my drift?"

"I think I do, Mr. Clark."

"It just seems like maybe there's something a little more for someone who doesn't mind working. Maybe make a little more money. Maybe somewhere you don't get punched in the eye at four in the morning."

"Maybe there is. But the factories are all the way out on the outskirts of town and I don't drive. I could walk in the summer, but I'd freeze to death in the winter."

"I guess that's true. Have you ever thought about learning how to drive?"

"I don't know anyone that owns a car to even try to learn."

"Your parents don't own a car?"

"No, sir. At least my mom doesn't. I don't really know my dad."

"Huh. Well, maybe think about it, Henry. I'd gladly write you a letter of recommendation. You always show up to work and that's about 99% of any job. Just showing up."

"I actually kind of like this job."

"That's fair. Nothing wrong with that. And I'm happy to have you here. I guess I should worry more about myself and stop pestering you."

"I appreciate your concern, Mr. Clark. I really do."

"You don't want to wake up one day at 68 years-old to find out you've lived your entire life without making any of your own decisions, Henry. I know that's pretty forward. But it's something I wish someone would have told me when I was younger."

He's moved around the racks now and made his way closer to where I'm still standing, hunched inside the cooler, so he doesn't have to shout. This takes me off guard. I'm not sure where all of this was coming from. I'm trying to figure out a response when he jumps back into it.

"I married the person I was supposed to marry. We had kids because that's what we thought we were supposed to do. I wanted to be a painter, but my family thought that was ridiculous, so I went to school. And then came the offer to teach back here in Brooksville and I thought I'd still have all summer to paint. But with the kids came more and more responsibilities and we needed more money so I picked up work in the summer and I stopped painting altogether."

"What did you paint?"

"Oh, anything. Bowls of fruit and naked people. Cars. Everything. I loved the feeling of the brush on the surface. I enjoyed painting houses. The exterior of them even. I did that during the summers in college and I loved it. I remember thinking I could do that for the rest of my life. But my parents were helping pay for me to go to school and there was no way they were paying for me to go to art school. I ended up a math teacher right back here in Brooksville. Exactly where I didn't want to be. I always hated math. I still do, come to think of it. Even more now that I'm retired."

"Why'd you come back?"

"I had graduated from college and the loans I had taken out were going to start coming due. My parents were both teachers here in town and they said they could get me in at the high school. I wanted to travel but there just wasn't any time. They were so excited when they were able to get me an interview. I went in thinking it would just be for a year or so. Just something to get me on my feet before heading out into the world. But then life happened and I just never left."

"You didn't want to be a teacher?"

"It had never even crossed my mind to become a teacher. And I was never big on kids. Especially other people's. But the opportunity fell into my lap. How could I say no? And then I got used to it, I guess. And here we are."

"I'd always assumed teachers had always wanted to be teachers. That's why they were there."

"Some did. And you can usually tell right off which ones. Always showing up early and leaving late. But for most of us, it was just something to do to pay the bills. At least where I taught. Did you go to school here in town? I don't remember ever seeing you."

"I did. I tried to go unnoticed as best I could. I never took any of your classes though."

"But you know what I'm talking about then. All of those coaches were mostly kids that couldn't wait to get right back to high school as soon as they could. I can't say much, I guess. I ended up doing the exact same thing. Anyway, the kids grew up and left and the house was empty again and I was getting close to retiring and I thought I would finally have time to paint. But then Meredith got sick. I spent the next three years caring for her, which I don't regret, but still, here I am: My wife is dead, my kids are gone, and I can't even hold a paintbrush anymore."

"How'd you end up with the store?"

"My wife's idea. It was supposed to be our retirement plan. Something to keep us busy and bring in a little money. When she died I couldn't bring myself to sell it. And now I just don't have anything else to do, but stand here and preach to you about my mistakes."

He stops talking for a beat, as if he's waiting for me to stop him. I don't say anything. The hum of the cooler seems to get louder for a moment, but I know it's just the silence turning up the volume on us. He starts talking again.

"I let it all happen. And it's not a bad life. I've been very fortunate in my 68 years. But I thought it would be easier than doing the starving artist thing. It turns out it's all a tough road no matter which way we go. We might as well do something we enjoy."

"Like pricing milk."

"Get the hell off of your knees, kid. These folks can figure out the milk for their damn selves."

"I'm all done, anyway."

"Hell. I'm sorry, Henry. Just don't let life slip by you, huh? That's all I'm trying to say. That stuff with the gun was scary."

Mr. Clark turns and heads to the back office to count up the money, leaving me standing in the aisle with the cooler door still open. I am daydreaming, thinking about how Mr. Clark just assumed everyone owned a car and knew how to drive when the front door dings. Mr. Clark yells from the office that there is a customer.

Chapter 22

Do you ever think about how many people would be affected if you didn't wake up tomorrow? Mine is two.

My mother would cry, I think. For a little while. But the tears would be more for herself than for me. The other would be Josh.

And that's it. Two.

How about you? Not to pry, I'm just wondering. If you can get past five, you can stop counting them and start counting yourself lucky. How have I existed on this earth for 28 years and only have two people that would be affected by my death?

One of them being my mother.

Chapter 23

"The Shriners pancake breakfast will take place this Saturday 7-10 AM at the Council On Aging Center .... Gertrude Lawson will be laid to rest at Oakwood Cemetery tomorrow morning at 8 AM. She was the daughter of Wilson and Blanche Lawson and a resident of Brooksville for her entire 86 years .... The Brooksville Volunteer Fire Department responded to a fire alarm last night at 806 Chippewa Avenue at 9:03 PM. It was declared a false alarm at 9:23 PM .... Thank you for tuning in with us today and don't touch that dial! Up next we have The Chordettes with their 1958 classic, 'Lollipop.' WQRC 97.3: THE HITS YOU MISS!"

We get three radio stations in town. WQRC is the local station with local news and the old confetti-and-soda-pop bullshit of the 50s and 60s.

There's also the country station that plays songs written by rich people pandering to the poor rural people by romanticizing life in towns like Brooksville. They never mention the devastating drug problems and poverty.

That leaves the classic rock radio station. I tried for a year to wake up to it, but if I had to hear "Bad To The Bone" one more time I was going to lose my mind. And while I'm sure AC-DC is a fine band, I don't think I need to hear "Back in Black" ever again.

Over on AM, preachers from the different churches in town try to convince you that their idea is the right one. That living in the middle of a cornfield is God's way. That you will be rewarded for your suffering. The child putting its hand onto a hot stove and getting burned. Except no lessons ever get learned. We just keep reaching up and putting our hands right back on the stove around here.

Winter is still in full force when I leave the apartment. I pull the drawstring tight on the hood of my winter coat and step out into the cold. I make a right out onto the sidewalk and head west before cutting south towards the cemetery where my grandparents are both buried. After my grandfather died, my grandmother sold her plot next to his and found something a little further away from him. She wasn't a religious woman, but I guess she didn't want to take any chances on running into the bastard again, just in case of an afterlife.

After a few minutes in the cold, my body adjusts and I even begin to sweat underneath my coat. I walk through the cemetery gates out into the rows of gravestones. I remember when I was young and my mom would yell at me for stepping on the flat ones. I remember thinking that gravestones were some of the most nonsensical things in the world and that I wasn't sure who or what I was disrespecting by stepping on a stone with someone I didn't know's name on it, but nothing has changed because I don't step on them now either.

I find my grandfather's grave out by the fence next to the county road that runs along the south side of the cemetery. I loosen the drawstrings on my coat and slide my hood down and feel the cold air against my face, now warm with sweat. I don't know what has drawn me here today, but I felt the need to come. Maybe this is what gravestones are for.

Chapter 24

Standing over my grandfather's grave I realize that even in death he has spread his fear and anger into me. What do you do when you are scared to death of the people and places that you came from? When every move you make seems to bring you closer to becoming the one thing you promised yourself you would never become. I can feel his anger living on inside of me. And even though it's pointed towards him, I'm afraid that he's just my scapegoat. I worry that if I ever did fall in love with someone that anger could be projected onto them. The thought of that turns my stomach and I speak out loud to try and organize my thoughts.

"The fact that your blood runs through my veins haunts me every single day. I am glad that you are dead. You brought nothing but fear and anger into this world. I am nothing like you," I hear myself say.

I can see my breath hanging in the air like my mother's cigarette smoke.

"I know these things are inside of me and I hate you for it. I hate that I have to carry these feelings and thoughts with me everywhere I go. That I live in fear of becoming you. Or even being anything like you."

My nose is running and I feel the heat of tears start to run down my face. My left ear still has a faint ringing that is made even more pronounced by the cold silence of the cemetery. Standing out here in the freezing cold talking to myself. And even in the act of anger against him I become a little more like him every single day.

Chapter 25

I woke up to the phone ringing. I was laying in the living room back behind the couch that served as my bedroom in my mother's apartment. It was late. I remember laying there pretending to be asleep because I could tell by the tone of my mother's voice that something was wrong. She kept asking "Where?" and "Why?" over and over again. Her voice kept rising and getting louder and then she would remember I was there and she would shrink back down to a whisper. I was 11 years old. I remember laying there on the twin-sized blow-up mattress that served as my bed for years.

I woke up on the ground most mornings from the slow leak that every air mattress ever made has.

He was getting old. And tired. Tired of making excuses for why his life hadn't gone the way he had hoped. My mother had been out of the house for a long time, and after she left he didn't have many other ways to displace his anger. He could yell at his wife, but he had learned he needed to stay out of her way too. She made the dinners, did the laundry, fixed him drinks. I think she was ready for him to die. She was tired too.

"Henry, I know it's late, but I have to go out. Will you be ok here by yourself?"

"What's going on, Mom? And yes, I'm fine. I'm 11 years old. I can take care of myself."

"I know you can. But it's late. You'll be safe here, right? "

"What's going on? I know that was Grandma on the phone. And it's late. What's wrong?"

"It's your Grandpa. I don't know. He's run off somewhere."

"Where did he go?"

"The sheriff called Grandma and said that he was out at the new reservoir, kind of wandering around."

"That's doesn't sound like an emergency, Mom."

"Well, apparently he has his shotgun with him. And he's just kind of, you know, walking around. I have to get out there and see."

"What's he doing with a gun?"

"I don't know, Henry. That's why I have to go out and see."

Even at 11 years old, I could tell the level of fear in my mother's voice wasn't matching the story my mother was giving me. But I could also tell now wasn't the time to push it. She needed to go. And I needed to stay.

"You just go back to sleep and I'll be back before you wake up, ok?"

Thinking back now this was the most motherly I had ever heard or would ever hear my mother's voice. There's a warmth to a mother's voice. One that my mother never learned to use. It came out now out of the pure urgency of the situation. I remember it feeling good, even though the situation was bad. Maybe that's part of what it is to be a mother. To make the bad stuff less terrible.

I laid there and listened. The door shut and a car pulled up. I heard the car door close and the engine revving as it drove away from our apartment. It was summertime. I remember it being warm. And quiet. I pulled the covers back over my head and thought about my grandfather out there wandering around with his shotgun in the dark. I worried for everyone else around him. He was not a good man. He also thought very highly of himself. A gun in his hands was not trouble for himself. It was trouble for everyone else.

The sheriff's operator had called my grandmother. She had told my grandmother that my grandfather was pacing around and talking to himself. Carrying on full conversations with no one but himself. Arguing and laughing. Asking questions and yelling the answers. He had told the sheriff that the only way he was putting that gun down was if he could see his wife. And being the sheriff in such a small community, the big city rules we see on television shows and in movies did not apply.

All the sheriff wanted to do is go home when his shift was over. His job was 96% driving around Brooksville and yelling at kids for skateboarding or laughing too loud in a public space. There was an actual law in the town that no more than three kids under the age of 18 could gather in a single public space. So when he stumbled on this situation, his only goal was to get my grandfather out of there as soon as possible. So he called my grandmother. Well, he called into the station on his radio and the operator called my grandmother and explained the little she knew of the situation to her and told her that she was needed. My grandmother then called my mother.

When my grandmother and my mother arrived at the reservoir after midnight, they were met by the sheriff and one local cop.

The sheriff explained to the two of them that all they wanted to do was go home. They weren't looking to arrest anyone. They just wanted everybody safe and sound back at home. Everyone agreed. Everyone except my grandfather who was now walking down the small hill from the water to the parking lot with the shotgun still in his hand.

I wasn't there. I was still asleep at home. Or trying to sleep. But from what my mother has told me, my grandfather walked down the hill like nothing was wrong. My mother, grandmother, the sheriff, and the cop were waiting at the bottom of the hill, thinking that the situation was about to resolve itself. As he walked closer, he smiled at my mother. Like he hadn't been expecting to see her. And from what she tells me, he walked up to the two of them and said hello. Casually. Like everything was fine. He stopped and stood there for a moment, smiling. My grandmother told him to get in the car and that they were heading home and they could talk about all this in the morning. My mother swears she saw tears in his eyes, but she tells this part of the story poorly. "I could swear he was crying" or "I could tell he had been crying," she always says. I can tell she's just trying to write a nice ending for herself. The villain righting his wrongs, and in the moment of truth, recognizing the error of his ways.

What happened was my grandfather stuck the shotgun underneath his chin and pulled the trigger. He never said any kind of goodbye. And that was that. There was immediate shock and confusion, I'm sure. But by the next morning when I woke up to my mother and grandmother talking quietly over instant coffee in the living room—while I'm sure they were still both in shock—it seemed like the worst had passed.

I pretended I was still asleep. I didn't know yet what had happened the night before, but I could sense the release of tension. I just laid there and listened for a while. There was calm in both their voices. My grandmother telling my mother how he had been talking to himself for years. My mother saying she had noticed, my grandmother questioning whether she should have done something more. In the end both of them agreeing it was most certainly neither one of their faults and that maybe it was for the best. A pause for a long hug when my grandmother left. The door closing with care.

I wouldn't get any of the real details for another couple years. When I pretended to wake up that morning, I rose slowly, making noise to let my mother know that I was awake. I walked slowly across the shag carpet. I gave my mother a short hug and said good morning.

She asked if I wanted a bowl of cereal.

I said I did.

The only other thing I remember is that we were out of milk.

Chapter 26

My grandmother was smiling at her husband's funeral. The funeral home was full and she was walking around talking with the folks who had come to say goodbye to her dead husband, to comfort her. There was a new grace about her. You could see the relief in her eyes.

My mother had a harder time. Her father had killed himself right in front of her. He was her father and her abuser. So many emotions all twisted up into that one human being. The word had gotten around town fast. And as I'm sure it is in every small town everywhere, everyone loves a good tragedy. People came out of the taproom's wood paneling for the parade of grief, for a taste of the excitement. Any excuse to connect yourself to the big event. I remember asking my mom who all of these people were and her saying they were old friends of her dad's with a dismissive wave of her hand. I remember a lot of the men wearing overalls and placing their hats on their chests when talking to my grandmother. And a lot of those same men were later hugging my mother and saying that if she needed anything that she could call them. I realize now that my mom was only 28 at the time and that those men were just using grief to try and get closer to my mother. At that age I wasn't sure what to feel, but I knew sadness wasn't what was happening. It all felt so empty and there was a rightness about that. There's no need to mourn people who did nothing but create pain and hardship for others while they were here on earth.

When nature and nurture are both houses engulfed in flames, where does that leave you?

Many people have kids, I would guess, in an attempt to connect themselves back to humanity and create some kind of roots for themselves. That's sort of how I came into existence. My mother trying to create a new and better reality for herself, right the wrongs done to her through me. But what if the child grows up and becomes a mirror. And the parent finds their own reflection staring back at them in the child's eyes, all their fears come to life, there, whether they like it or not.

Chapter 27

"He put a brick through the guy's fucking head, Henry. Right out there on the sidewalk. He was like a wild animal. There were six of us out there trying to get him to stop, but he just kept swinging. I'd guess Kevin was dead after the first couple of minutes. But Nicky just kept on and on and on. The fucking blood was everywhere. When the cops pulled up, I think the sirens brought him back to reality and he realized what he had done. He slumped back and let his head just hang there. And then he started crying. When he finally let the brick fall from his hands it fell in three different pieces. The thing had broken while he was beating Kevin and he had been holding it together in his hand. The cops started trying to clear us out while they cuffed Nicky and got him into the back of the cop car. There was nothing left to even try mouth-to-mouth on. Kevin's head was like a deflated balloon. I can't unsee it."

I don't want to hear this, but I can't stop Steve from talking.

"I mean, Nicky just lost it. I guess Kevin had been calling Nicky's girlfriend while he was in county. Damn, Henry. I'm not going to be able to sleep tonight. It makes me sick to my stomach just thinking about it."

"And Nicky had one of those ankle monitors on that parole officers use to keep track of folks. The thing kept beeping like a fire alarm the entire time. Kevin's brother was there, too. He saw the whole damned thing."

"Did you close early? It's only one now."

"Nah. Natalie's closing for me tonight. I had to get out of there."

"Pack of Reds?"

"Better make it two. I've got a feeling it's going to be a long night, Henry."

I knew something was up when I heard the sirens coming from different directions. There aren't many cops in town, so if you hear more than two sirens that means they've called in reinforcements from the county. The fire department is all volunteer, so just like with the cops, if you see more than one fire truck you know something big is happening. It's no false alarm. I had seen two cop cars and two sheriff cars from out in the county go flying down the street from behind the counter. I knew it wouldn't take long to hear the news.

I'd always assumed that Nicky Halcourt would kill someone. The kids that had grown up with him had watched him go from a small-time bully into a full-blown maniac in the span of a few years.

One day he was stealing lunch money from the sixth-graders, and the next he was pummeling anyone who dared to speak to him. We had heard the stories from our parents. His dad was a drunk and his mom had left him there to contend with his father all by himself. I remember him showing up to school with black eyes, broken arms, occasional crutches. And then sometime during our sophomore year the injuries stopped. None of us put it together until later, but Nicky had hit a growth spurt.

He learned how to fight from his dad. No pulling punches not wanting to hurt your best friend. Nicky was a swing-to-kill, prison-rules fighter since he was a kid. Most people never really learn to fight like that. No matter how mad we are we have a gauge inside of us that stops us from actually wanting to hurt one another. Nicky had no such gauge. Once during our senior year, Nicky got hold of Mr. Simms, our gym teacher, after he had called Nicky a loser in front of the class. Nicky hit him in a way I had never witnessed in real life. It was a punch with purpose. And that purpose was to kill Mr. Simms. Lucky for Mr. Simms, the punch had only knocked him unconscious and sent him crashing through the trophy case next to the locker rooms. Everyone had stood there, stunned waiting to see what happened next. Nicky knew the score, he walked straight out of the school, never to return.

When the word got around that Nicky wasn't coming back everyone—teachers and students—breathed a little sigh of relief.

Mr. Simms did return. He spent the rest of the year punishing us for his embarrassment.

As for Kevin, I would never wish any kind of harm on anyone—let alone being beaten to death with a brick on a sidewalk outside of a bar—but the genuine mourners of his death would probably fit in a broom closet, comfortably.

I can see it already. At the funeral they will tell some stories that have very little relevance to the person that Kevin ever was. They'll stuff some religious filler in to beef up the service. His mother will cry. His father will not. His brother will bring his new girlfriend and be ready to go before they even get there. This is what real life looks like.

Some of us just die. No fanfare. No one slamming their fists against the casket claiming it wasn't his time.

And the world just keeps turning.

Chapter 28

In the morning when I get off work I still can't shake the vision of Nicky slamming that brick into Kevin's skull. It's still quiet outside. The occasional car passes with a cloud of hot exhaust hanging closely behind it. I tell myself to take the long way home, bypassing the scene of the incident, but my legs don't listen. I make the left off of Main Street and there I am in front of the Angry Steer.

The dried blood is all over the sidewalk. The stain spreads out into the street. The biggest, darkest blood spot speaks pretty loudly. As does the jukebox that is still playing inside the bar. I can hear excited voices inside retelling the details to the third-shift folks who are here having drinks after work.

I peer into the bar through the small octagon window next to the front door. Past the neon beer sign, I see them all lined up on their stools. My breath is fogging the window and I reach up to wipe it clean.

There's no one here crying over Kevin McCarthy. No memorial candles or grocery store flowers. Just a blood stain on an early morning sidewalk and a new story to tell to the regulars.

In a few hours someone from the city will come along and spray Kevin's blood out into the street and into the storm drain.

A wet, heavy snow starts to fall from a grey sky. I stuff my hands deep into my coat pockets and start my way home.

Chapter 29

My mom called me at work last night to tell me that she had today off and maybe it would be good if I came over and saw her. We have opposite schedules so these things have to be planned. And after the events of last night I welcomed the thought of seeing her.

The walk to my mom's apartment from mine is less than a mile. I walk past double-wide trailers stuck on small muddy lots, almost all of them with satellite dishes stuck on the southwest corners and cardboard covering broken windows. I can feel the plastic door handles on the cheap hollow doors in the palm of my hand. The smell of hot-plate meals that gets baked into the carpets. Neighborhood kids play outside with no coats on. Dogs tied to ropes connected to the bumpers of cars bark and growl as I walk by. There's so much sadness here. You can feel it in the air. The desperation is bubbling over and no end in sight.

My mother's place is a one-bedroom apartment on the first floor of a six-apartment complex. She has an end unit, which means she only has to contend with one shared wall. She hates that the neighbor's baby screams at all hours, but they don't complain about the volume of her TV or her smoking inside so she doesn't complain about the baby.

I walk up the sidewalk to her front door and see she still has her Christmas lights and decorations in her front window and a wreath exclaiming, "Merry Christmas!" with Santa Claus in his sleigh. She's had this wreath for as long as I can remember. There used to be reindeer connected to the sleigh, but I accidentally broke them off pulling it out of the box sometime in my teens.

I knock lightly, knowing that she'll be sitting on the couch, in her bathrobe, watching TV. I hear her yell for me to come in.

"Henry, come on in."

"Hey Mom, I brought donuts."

"Thank you! Just set them on the counter there."

"You look good today," I tell her.

"You're just being nice, but thank you. I didn't feel like getting dressed this morning and by the time I looked up from the TV it was already the afternoon. I've got no one to impress anyway, so what's the difference."

The inside of her apartment is sparse. Couch and TV in the living room with a small table in between covered in change, a few loose dollar bills, empty cigarette packs, and an ashtray with a palm tree sticking up from it and a female figure standing next to the tree wearing a red bikini and white sunglasses, the word FLORIDA printed in bright orange on the brown base.

As a child of the 80s in a single-parent home, I was raised on TV. It was babysitter, teacher, and time-waster, a constant companion. I used to think this was specific to me, but now it seems like it's a generational thing. It's why I don't have a TV in my apartment. I could sit and watch crime shows for hours without blinking an eye. I figure I don't need anything that helps me be even more complacent and distanced from reality than I've already become.

My back is to the screen, but I can tell which detective is speaking without looking.

My mother looks tired. Not the kind of tired you look from staying up too late or drinking too much, but the kind of tired one can only get from a life lived not knowing where your next meal is coming from. Or if you're going to be able to make rent. It's a level of exhaustion someone with money could never understand.

She hasn't always been like this. She used to have some fight inside of her. Similar to Mel at work. Anger, laughter, sadness, and fear. Sometimes all at the same time. But when my grandmother died the light started to fade. They had spent the years after my grandfather had died getting closer and catching up on lost time, but there was always some resentment for the way my mother's father had treated her and the fact that her mother never spoken up. That she had allowed things to go on the way they did until my mother simply had to leave. I don't believe they ever spoke of it outright, so the bridge was never built between them. You can feel these distances in your heart.

My grandmother's funeral had been sparse. Nothing like my grandfather's. No outpouring of sudden goodwill from strangers. No tragedy for everyone to come get the inside scoop on. Just a woman who had been fighting for her life since the day she met her husband. She had come out victorious in the end. Sort of. She finally got to be a mother to her daughter and less of a protector and more of a grandmother to me. Those days are a nice memory in the midst of a chaotic childhood now, but I didn't know that at the time.

"Well, hey, why don't you bring us those donuts? There's a two-liter of Coke in the fridge. Grab it. Your favorite detective is just wrapping this case up, but there's a marathon on Channel 9. Mostly the older ones, but those are my favorites."

I walk to the kitchen and grab two Christmas-themed Coca-Cola promotional glasses out of the cabinet and fill them with ice. I grab the soda from the fridge and the box of donuts off the kitchen counter. I slide the box onto the small table between the couch and the TV, careful not to disrupt the ashtray. I set down the glasses and soda bottle. I take a seat next to my mother and we each eat three glazed donuts and wash them down with flat Coke while watching the detective clean up the case in the 42 minutes allowed him by network TV.

Chapter 30

The Brooksville Lamplight: Stay informed!

HOTEL DESK CLERK NEEDED

- High school diploma or equivalent preferred
- Competitive wages
- Apply at Smith's Inn today! (ask for Cindy)

DO YOU NEED CASH FAST?

- Do you consider yourself a people person?
- Do new challenges excite you?
- Previous phone skills preferred
- Apply today at BKS Technologies!

BKS Technologies?

These are call centers. They are always call centers. Selling diet pills and time-shares to senior citizens over the phone.

I tried it once right after high school. The only thing more depressing than the job was how many people actually bought the stuff. Mostly to have someone to talk to.

419 LUMBER

- Starting at $11.00 an hour
- Must be able to work weekends
- Reliable transportation a must

Lights and Sirens

— A lost dog was reported on W. Spring St.

— A suspicious person was reported on E. Irving. BPD responded to call; no contact was made.

— A wallet was reported lost. Owner later reported wallet found on top of car.

***

The front door bell dings and I look up from the paper to see Steve walking in.

"The ole *Lamplight*, huh? Intriguing stuff."

"Hey, Steve. How are things?"

"It's been pretty quiet since the whole murder thing."

"Yeah. That can put a damper on the party.

"I think everyone stops for a minute to take stock, ya know? Makes you stop and think."

"Definitely. How about you, Steve?"

"I'm ok. The first few days were tough. Trying to forget something like that isn't easy. I stayed home for a couple days and hung around with the kids. That's seemed to help the most. Trying to bring life back into perspective a little. I'm ok. They're ok. That's all that matters to me."

"I've been taking a little mental inventory myself."

"Yeah? How's it looking?"

"It turns out I'm not doing so great. And I might be kind of an asshole."

"You are. But that's why I like ya."

"Thanks?"

"It's alright, man. I thought you knew? I thought that was like, your thing."

"Always the last to know. "

"It's nothing personal. You were always different. And you kind of held it over everyone."

"So I'm the asshole, anti-social convenience store clerk?"

"Sort of. I enjoy it. I like having someone to bitch about these assholes with. Just don't forget we're both those assholes, too. You've always kept to yourself unless it was to sit on someone or something. This town, the people. And it's funny. But we're not 12 anymore. We're all grown up. And here you are. It's 3 AM and you're selling me cigarettes .... I'm not trying to be a jerk, here. "

"Thanks for the honesty."

"If you hate all of this so much, you should just go."

"That's easier said than done."

"There is and always will be a million reasons to not do something, Henry."

"Where's all of this wisdom coming from tonight?"

"Vodka and Captain Red."

"What's Captain Red?"

"Some generic energy drink. Comes out of the soda gun at the bar. Poor man's speedball. I had three and now I'll be awake until the sun comes up."

"$5.63 for the smokes. Any parting words of wisdom, Captain Red?"

"Thanks, Henry. You know, this might be news to you, but not everyone is miserable here. Some of us really like it. I can own the bar and have a house and raise a family. My commute is six minutes if I take the long way. And yeah, there are a lot of assholes here, but there are a lot of assholes everywhere. You don't like it here, and that's ok, too. But you sitting here ringing up boner pills and whatever the fuck this is ...."

"It's a Murple."

"What the fuck's a .... it doesn't matter. My point is that you sitting here night in and night out being unhappy doesn't do anyone any good .... Sorry, man. This Captain Red is really doing a number on me."

"I'm sorry if I was an ass to you."

"Nah. Like I said, I always liked you, Henry."

"Thanks."

"Have a good night, Henry. Stay safe in here."

"Thanks Steve. Be safe getting home."

"No sweat. My cousin Rick is the only cop on duty right now. "

"Small-town charm, huh?"

"You know it ... and Henry, stop in for a drink sometime. On me."

Chapter 31

Steve walks out the door and I hear him say hello to someone as the door's closing. It almost closes when the bell dings again before I can pick the paper back up.

"Buy something and get out or I'm calling the cops, Gina."

"What's got into you tonight?"

"Really? You have to ask?"

"Yeah. What's stuck in your craw?"

"Umm, you punched me in the face the last time you were in here. Sorry if I'm a little defensive."

"Shit. I'm sorry, Henry. I've been a little fucked up lately. I'm really sorry. Can I just use the bathroom real quick?"

"Seriously?" I say in a tone in disbelief while trying to decide if it's worth the fight. Her brazenness surprises me even as it pisses me off.

"Please, Henry? I'm really sorry about the other night. I really need to use the bathroom."

She seems genuinely sorry and I decide it isn't worth getting punched over again.

"Yeah, go for it."

I hand her the women's room key that's connected to an old license plate. It's ridiculous, but Mr. Clark insists upon it.

"Thanks, Henry!" Gina says. She grabs the key from my hand and runs to the restroom.

When she reappears, her arms are wrapped around her torso and her forehead is covered in sweat.

"Thanks," she says as she sets the license plate and key down on the counter with a clunk.

"Hey, have you seen Ricky lately?"

"Really, come on. You two are my absolute least favorite couple in the whole wide convenience store world."

"What's he ever done to you? Ricky really likes you."

"Is that why he tried to shoot me?"

"What are you talking about?"

"He really didn't mention to you that he came in here waving his dad's gun around again and the thing went off?"

"No. He didn't tell me anything about that. Are you serious?"

"Dead serious. And I haven't seen him in days. And I like it that way. "

"I'm sorry if I was an asshole to you. And if he comes in just please tell him I'm looking for him. It's important."

6:54 AM

"I guess you haven't cleaned the women's room yet?"

"I haven't. It was super busy this morning. I was gonna do it before I left. What's wrong?"

"I don't get paid enough for this shit."

"That bad? I'll take care of it, Mel. Just let me finish counting my drawer down."

"I don't think you wanna go in there, Henry. Just finish counting out and cover the counter for a few, will ya?"

"Of course. What's going on in there?"

"Well, as far as I can tell someone lost a baby in there last night. Or what would have been a baby. It might be a little bit too much for you to handle."

"Gina. The woman that punched me in the face. She came in asking to use the restroom last night."

"Was she the only one?"

"I think so."

"Well, your friend Gina could probably use a friend today. Or a drink."

Mel was standing with the women's room door open looking in. I walked over and stood next to her.

I went to step in, but hesitated. There was blood around the toilet seat and on the ground. When I looked inside I saw what looked to me like a small bloody mouse inside the toilet bowl. But I knew it wasn't.

I walked out of the bathroom and heard Mel asking if I was ok. I yelled back that I just needed some air. On the way out I grabbed a pack of cigarettes and a lighter from the counter.

It was still dark out but the sky was starting to turn pink on the edges. I unwrapped the box and pulled a cigarette out and lit it up. I inhaled deep and exhaled slowly. It was cold and the smoke mixed with my breath in the morning air. I could hear my heart beating in my ears.

"It's for the best," I said out loud to myself.

Everyone involved was better off this way. Mel and I could do our little part knowing that this was the smallest mess that could have come from the situation.

I thought of my mother and of myself. This entire mess we call our lives. And I couldn't help but think that neither Gina nor that little red blob would ever know how lucky they really were.

Chapter 32

Josh,

What do you do with the idea that you weren't supposed to be here? That maybe you're not emotionally or mentally equipped to live in the world as it is?

It's times like these I actually understand religion. And why it's so popular in places like Brooksville. It gives some kind of order to the chaos. Like your life isn't completely meaningless. The problem is that none of that changes the reality of the situation. My friend Marge said life is just a game, but that doesn't make the pain any less real. Our pain or the pain we inflict upon others.

Remember a few years ago this guy went out to Smith's where his wife was waitressing and shot her right in the dining room of the restaurant? What are we supposed to do with that kind of information? If that's the game then I'm not sure I want to play. And it's not like I want to die, I'm just not sure living is for me. I'm sorry I always write you when I'm feeling like this. It helps me get outside of my own head when I can share these thoughts and feelings with someone who might understand.

As for this Captain Jane/Memory Currency situation, I'm still not seeing any greater metaphor or meaning behind any of it. I went back and read the first couple of issues again and it does help give a little more context to the situation. The first page in the first issue is a kid sitting in his room inside of a thought bubble of the artist sitting at a desk drawing Captain Jane. It seems that the artist is just making these things up and we're just supposed to roll with it. I dug a few more of the older issues out and I'm going to go over them and see what else we missed all those years ago. I'll let you know what I find out.

I hope you're doing well.

Your friend,

Henry

Dear Henry,

I understand what you're saying, but I'm afraid I don't have the answers to any of these questions. What I think is that none of us are really supposed to be here, not any more than anyone else. It's important to remember that you are just as equipped as everyone else to handle life. It's not easy for anyone. We're all out here struggling. It's also important to remember to not get addicted to the struggle. Your troubles don't go away when you move to a new place. But a new place can give you a whole new perspective on life. You don't have to live in the wake of the people that created you. You can make your own wake.

It would be really great if you could make it down soon. It seems like you could stand to get away from the convenience-store business for a little while. You're always welcome here. And don't' worry, I enjoy your darkness sometimes. Just don't be afraid of a little light every once in a while.

I had forgotten all about the first issues of Memory Currency! I mean, I knew they existed but I didn't remember there being any kind of set-up like you mentioned in your letter. Let me know what else I missed. I'm going to try and track down some old issues at the library here. I keep rereading the last two issues and I really think there's something more there.
Let's talk soon.

Your friend,

Josh

Chapter 33

I make a left out my front door and head east towards Main Street. When I get to Main, I make a right and head south towards the coffee shop. It's still cold outside but the wind that usually blows down from the north has relaxed a bit and I'm able to keep my face exposed and breathe freely without it being painful. I'm wearing a pair of leather gloves I took from the lost-and-found box at work. They'd been sitting there since last winter and no one had come around asking about them. I figured anyone with a pair of gloves this nice was probably able to go out and buy a new pair when they lost their old ones, so I didn't think too much about it. You could tell that they were expensive from the softness of the leather. And the inside of them was lined with some kind of fur. I'm not sure if it was real animal fur or not, but it felt really nice. When I brought them home it occurred to me that the gloves were probably the most expensive thing I owned. They were definitely the most expensive article of clothing I had ever owned. They almost made me wish that winter would stick around a little longer. I was going to have a hard time putting them away when the warmer weather finally arrived.

At the town square, I stop at the light and wait for it to change so I can cross. The light changes and I take one step out into the street when I hear the screech of tires and a thick thump that makes me recoil back onto the sidewalk.

An early 90s Nissan Sentra is stopped in the crosswalk. The driver's side door is covered in black spray paint. The rest of the car is gold spray paint, with gray primer showing beneath. I stand still on the sidewalk, confused about what has just happened when the driver gets out and starts screaming for help. He's young. Early twenties, I'd say. He's wearing a white thermal shirt underneath a black Nine Inch Nails t-shirt. He has a baseball cap on backwards with an energy drink logo emblazoned on the front which is facing towards me. He looks under the car and screams "Fuck!"

I run as fast as I can towards him. He has a look of pure terror on his face.

He screams at me, "She came out of fucking nowhere, man!"

I yell at him to turn the car off and I slide underneath the front end of the car and see the little girl lying there.

"Am I ok?," she asks.

"You're ok .... you're ok," I answer, trying to sound calm and confident.

There are some situations in this world where the truth doesn't help anyone involved.

The driver is standing over me hyperventilating and trying to give me his side of the story. I slide out from under the car and get to my feet and grab the keys from his hand.

The little girl was underneath the car, but not the wheels. I yell at the driver that we need to move the car away from her without starting it. I don't know if that's possible, but it seems like the only thing to do. The driver gets in and I watch him carefully turn the key one click over. I scream at the driver to shock him out of the verbal courtroom defense he's still pleading while sitting in the driver's seat. I go to the front of the car and start to push as hard as I can. The driver hops out and helps me push the car back far enough so that the car is no longer hovering over top of the little girl.

Her hand-me-down adult-sized coat is splayed on the ground, much too thin for February in Ohio. One silver snow boot on her right foot is pointed towards the sky (Why do people's shoes always pop off when they get hit by cars?). Her bootless left foot and leg are twisted in a way that's unnatural.

I ask her names, but she keeps saying "Mommy" over and over again.

I catch her mangled leg on the frozen concrete in my periphery vision as I slide my left hand under her head and pull it toward my chest. I feel a sticky wetness on the back of her head, even through my leather glove. I pull her tighter.

I sit in the street holding her as the sirens begin to close in around us. I'm glad that someone has seen what is going on and thought to call 911. I keep asking what her name is and does she know where she lives and what her mommy's name is, but she isn't talking anymore.

My mind is buzzing and my vision is a direct tunnel between the little girl and I. I've watched enough crime shows to know that I shouldn't have picked her up or moved her in any way. I know that. But that's not what I did. I couldn't just let her lay here in this street with cars passing by and the world continuing to spin.

I start to sing, softly.

"This little light of mine, I'm gonna let it shine. This little light of mine, I'm gonna let it shine."

She seems to weigh more now than when I picked her up. The dark spot on the pavement. The blood now pooling in my hand holding her head.

"This little light of mine, I'm gonna let it shine."

The sirens are splitting my eardrums now and the lights are flashing all around us and we seem to be surrounded, but no one else is offering help as I'm frantically rocking her back and forth in the middle of the street.

"Let it shine, let it shine, let it shine."

Chapter 34

The next thing I remember is sitting in the back seat of a cop car with my face pressed against the window. It's started snowing a wet, fat flake snow. I peel my forehead from the cold window. The cop and I catch each other's glance in his rearview mirror. She looks young. Younger than me, at least. I look down at my gloves, now covered in blood. It's all over my pants and coat too. The sight of it makes me want to throw up, but I take a deep breath and try to concentrate on my breathing. The feeling of my body inhaling and exhaling. I don't remember getting in the car or telling her where I lived, but I must have because we come to a stop in front of my apartment.

"Is this you?"

"Umm, yeah. That's me."

"You gonna be okay?"

"I have no idea."

"I'm sorry you had to see that. "

"Is she dead?"

"They got her to the hospital pretty quick. Hopefully she'll pull through."

"I think she died. While I was holding her. She was talking at first, but then she just went quiet. I didn't know what to do so I just held her. I know I shouldn't have moved her, but she was just laying there in the street …."

My voice is no longer connected to me. I hear myself speaking, but I have no control over what is coming out.

"It was so cold. I couldn't just let her lay there."

My voice rises in pitch. I feel warm snot running out of my nose onto my lip as the disconnected high-pitch voice gets louder and higher.

"I didn't kill her, did I? By moving her?"

My voice is a dog whistle.

"Hey, it's ok. She'll be ok. You're gonna be ok," the cop says to me as our eyes meet again in the rearview mirror.

She takes a deep, uncomfortable breath and reaches into her puffy, black cop jacket with a gold patch in the shape of a shield on the right arm.

"Here, take this. It's my card," she says, reaching back and sliding it through the fencing that separates the front and back seats. She has to fold the card into a cylinder to fit it through the cage.

"If you need anything, someone to talk to or anything, you just call me and I can set you up with someone who can help. Ok? You're gonna be alright. I know it's hard seeing shit like this, but you get past it. You'll be alright."

I take another deep breath and try and pull myself together enough to at least get out of the car. I clear my throat, trying to get my voice back to a normal pitch.

"I'm sorry. I kind of lost it there. Thank you."

I take her card and thank her no less than six more times as I search for the door handle to get out of the back seat.

"I have to let you out," she says.

She gets out, walks around the car, and opens up my door. I pull myself out of the hard plastic back seat of the cop car, again promising that I'll be ok, that I'm fine, really, just a little shook up.

Suddenly self-aware again, I can't get away from her or the car fast enough. I am halfway to my front door when I hear her yell from the car.

"Seriously, if you need anything. Just call."

"Thank you. I will," I say, waving the card in the air above my head.

She waves and drives away.

My hands are shaking as I try to fit the key into the lock of the front door. I have to steady my right hand with the key in it with my left before finally sliding it into the lock. My new leather gloves are still sticky with blood.

When I step inside I immediately shake the gloves off of my hands and onto the floor. I rip my coat off and pull at my shirt. I struggle with my belt buckle and stumble into the kitchen hopping on one foot while trying to get my jeans off. I throw my socks into the trashcan next to the refrigerator.

Standing naked at the kitchen sink I scrub the blood from my hands. I watch the water turn pink as it runs down the drain, replaying the scene over and over in my head. Telling myself what I should have done differently. The water turns less and less pink until it finally runs clear. The last of the little girl's blood runs from my hands and down the drain and through the pipes as I stand naked in the kitchen, talking to myself and wishing there was a god so at least I'd have someone to blame besides myself.

I walk into the bathroom and start the shower. I turn the knob all the way to the left. I sit naked on the toilet seat letting the steam fill the room before getting in. I need the water as close to boiling as it can get. There's not enough soap in the world to wash this blood off my body or the scene from my mind.

When I finish showering, my skin is pink and raw. It hurts to touch, but I feel better than I did before I got in. I walk into my bedroom and fall face first onto the futon mattress on the floor. I dream of that little girl and her twisted leg and lifeless body on a loop until 10:07 PM.

Chapter 35

Walking to work that night I keep clear of the scene of the accident. I walk three blocks south before turning left and heading east to Main Street. It all happened just a few hours ago, but it seems like weeks have gone by. I keep seeing her face and hearing her voice asking for her mother. The feel of that little girl in my arms. I thought about going to the hospital to try and check on her, but I didn't think it was my place to be there. The family would have enough to deal with without me hanging around looking for forgiveness. I knew that if I went to work the newspaper would show up around 5 AM and the accident would maybe make the morning paper. The chances were slim but, dead or alive, I needed to know.

The store is empty when I arrive except for Mel sitting behind the counter doing her end-of-shift count.

"Hey Henry, how are you tonight?"

"What are you doing here, Mel?"

"Kristy called in this afternoon and asked if I'd cover her shift. I could use the money so I said yes. Same as always. Gotta get home and get to sleep to do it all again tomorrow. Did you hear about that little girl downtown today?"

"I was there."

"Seriously?"

"I think the guy blew a red light."

"Was she okay? I heard she got hit but no one knew much more than that."

"I don't know. I don't think so. She didn't seem ok."

"Jesus, Henry."

"I was across the street. I ran over to see what happened and I could see her feet sticking out from under the car. Her leg was pretty twisted up. I don't know."

Hearing these words coming out of my mouth makes my eyes well up with tears. You think you're processing things in your mind, but when you say it out loud it's like hearing it for the first time again. Like the sound of your own words out loud turns your thoughts into reality.

"She goes to school with my daughter. I got scared when one of the customers told me and I called home to check on my kids and make sure they were all ok."

"You don't know her name, do you?

"Damn, the baby-sitter told me but I was so relieved that they were ok I wasn't really paying attention. What did you do?"

"I made the driver move the car and then I sat there with her and held her. She kept asking for her mom. I asked her what her mom's name was and where she lived but she just kept saying Mommy."

"Was she still alive when the cops showed up?"

"She had stopped talking and she had gotten real heavy by the time the ambulance got there. It felt like it took forever."

"Are you sure you're going to be ok in here tonight? Want me to call Randy, see if he'll come in and cover for you?"

"Don't bother him. If I'm not here I'm just going to be at home driving myself crazy. I'd rather have some kind of distraction."

"Did they tell you anything? The cops? EMTs?"

"The cop who gave me a ride home gave me her card, said I could call her."

"I can stick around for a little bit if you want to talk about it."

"I appreciate that, but you can go. You've been here all day. I'm hoping there will be something in the paper."

"Well, kids are tough, Henry, believe me. I've watched mine fall from trees and all kinds of crazy shit. They're built to live."

"I hope so. Your numbers all good for the night?"

"Yeah, it's all here. Some kid came in here and put a bottle of Mountain Dew in his jacket and I was too tired to mess with it, I just wrote it off as waste."

"Gotcha. That it?"

"That's it. You sure you'll be okay?"

"Yeah, I'll be fine. "

Mel was using her mother tone with me. It felt good. She wasn't all that much older than me, but with all the life she had seen and along with being an actual mother, she had that tone. It could convince you things were going to be okay even when they weren't. I needed it right now.

"You did a good thing today, Henry. Being there for that little girl. You did good by her."

Then she leaned in and hugged me. Up close, her perfume smelled like candy. It amazed me how compassionate Mel could be, how she could just slip into it. One minute she's telling someone to go fuck themselves over the price of a Slurpee and the next she's a glowing orb of motherly love. I hoped that this person was the one that went home to her kids.

We're forced by life to become tough. To put up walls around ourselves. It's unfortunate that so often our lot in life forces us to protect ourselves from the world around us. We turn into harsh, sarcastic caricatures of ourselves. We teach ourselves to be mean as a way to walk through the world a little easier. But in the end it just leaves us even worse off.

"Take care of yourself, Henry. I'll see you in the morning."

"Sounds good, Mel. And thank you. I needed that."

"We all do, Henry. We all do."

Chapter 36

I feel the cold rush in through the door as Mel walks out and into the February night. I think of my brain making new pathways connecting her scent to love and warmth. Making a new memory. A positive one. How she probably hates the smell of that perfume, but she wears it because it was a gift from her kids for her birthday or Christmas. It's the kind of scent that kids would buy, never thinking that maybe their mom wouldn't want to be out in the adult world smelling like artificial watermelon or strawberry all day. Kids don't have to think about those things.

It's unfortunate that it's in tragedy we find ourselves at our most human. Our most beautiful moments seem to come out of darkness. If we could only learn to carry just a little bit of that humanity with us throughout our everyday.

I walk over to the ice cream cooler that stands waist-high near the far side of the front counter. After careful inspection I push the right sliding door over, reach in and pull a Drumstick out from the bottom right corner of the box. I brush away some icicles. Back behind the counter, I sit down on the stool, reach under the register, and pick up the waste sheet and the copy of *Memory Currency* I keep here at work. I mark the Drumstick off as waste, pull open the wrapper, and turn to page seven of *Memory Currency*. When I look up at the clock it's almost midnight.

The digital DJ is cueing up the 12 AM Star Spangled Banner and I have five more hours until the paper comes. Seven more hours until I can go directly to the hospital.

Chapter 37

When the front door bell dings and the paper delivery guy opens the door at 5 AM, I'm in the back of the store mopping the floor. I drop the mop and come up front to meet him. I take the stack of papers from his arms and tell him I'll take care of them. He thanks me and heads back outside to the white-panel van that's still running at the curb, just outside the door. I set the stack of papers on the counter and find a pair of scissors to cut the yellow plastic strips binding them together. I search every inch of the paper for any mention of the accident.

After three times through I realize there's nothing here. The accident must have been too late in the day to make today's paper. Disheartened, I fold the paper back together, put it back in the stack, and place the stack in the rack by the front door. I walk back to the mop bucket and try finishing the floor, but I can't focus on anything aside from getting to the hospital as soon as possible. I force myself to finish mopping, but abandon arranging the milk cooler. I start counting my drawer down at six-thirty. I yell a goodbye over my shoulder to Mel as I walk out the door at six fifty-nine.

It's about a two-and-a-half mile walk to the hospital from the store, but I make it in what would be record time if anyone were to keep records of such a thing. I'm half-running as I climb Hospital Hill when I feel the snot freezing on my face. I slow down and wipe my nose, taking a moment to catch my breath.

I walk through the revolving door at the front of the hospital into the fluorescent lights and I'm hit instantly with the smell of industrial sanitizer and chicken and peas being cooked by steam. Fluorescent lights are never anywhere that you actually want to be. School, offices, hospitals, interrogation rooms in prisons on TV. They make even the healthiest person look that sickening gray green.

I find the front desk, make a beeline to it. There's a man sitting there, seemingly ready to help. I try to speak calmly, but it comes out as much more of a demand than I intend.

"I'm here about the little girl that was hit by a car downtown yesterday."

The man is startled by my sudden appearance and it takes a moment for him to register my presence. He sets his pen down and removes a pair of thin, silver-framed reading glasses that now hang around his neck by a small gold beaded chain.

“Are you family?,” he says in a not too friendly tone, which is understandable. The urgency of the situation hasn’t left much room for nuance.

“I’m not,” I confess.

“I’m sorry, but we’re not allowed to give out information on patients to anyone that is not immediate family.”

“Ok, but I was hoping that maybe you could tell me, well, anything. I was there when the accident happened. When she got hit by the car. I just wanted to know if she was alright. And I’m sorry that came out so aggressive. I just walked here from work and I’m worried is all.”

“I’m sorry, but I’m not allowed to give out that information, sir.”

I hear my mother’s calming sigh come from my mouth.

I try walking away but I can’t let go of the desk. My grip tightens on the edge of it. The heat rises in my face. I feel the constant ache of winter in all of my extremities. The heavy, gray sadness of it feeds my misplaced anger and frustration with the situation.

My voice turns to pleading.

“Please sir, from one human to another. I told her that her mother was coming. I held her in the street after it happened. I moved her and I know I shouldn't have, but I didn't know what else to do. I just need to know if she's ok."

Tears begin streaming down my face and I can't seem to get air in and out of my lungs. Soon, I'm sobbing uncontrollably. I cry for the girl, for myself, for everyone involved really, for the poor guy sitting in front of me having to deal with life and death every single day for just a few more bucks than what I make selling lottery tickets and microwaved hamburgers.

I look up at the ceiling and into the fluorescent lights while trying to calm myself. I think of what a mess I must look like.

I stand there trying to get some kind of control over myself. The receptionist looks at me and sighs. He swivels in his chair, picks up his pen, and starts writing. He folds up a pink Post-It note and goes to hand it to me. When I reach for it, he holds onto to it for a moment and looks me in the eye. He speaks.

"Are you gonna be ok?"

"I'm sorry. I'm just tired."

"Ok," he says, and lets go of the Post-It note.

"You should probably get out of here."

I say the most sincere thank you I can manage and jam the fist holding the Post-it into my jacket pocket.

I turn and see the natural light pouring through the front doors and walk towards it. I push my way through the revolving door and into the morning sunlight. I take a deep breath of winter air into my lungs and pull paper from my pocket and unfold it.

"She didn't make it. I'm sorry," is what it says.

Chapter 38

I think I had already knew but I needed someone to tell me for certain. She had died right there in the street as I held her. I had felt it. One minute she was alive and the next ... gone.

"Hey man, do you have a cigarette I can bum?"

I turn around to see a skinny, withered man standing next to me. Way beyond what any reasonable human would call a suntan. He was cooked. Like his bones had already started to bleach. He had long hair sticking out all over his head and his teeth were broken and discolored from years of nicotine. His face was cracked leather and he had sunglasses on the top of his head and was wearing a Rolling Stones t-shirt. The one with the lips on it with the tongue sticking out.

"Sorry, I don't smoke."

"Know where I can get a beer? This place is killing me. I had to get out of there."

"There are a couple of places downtown that should be open."

"Could you give me a lift? It's cold as hell out here."

"I walked here. You don't have a coat?"

"I said goodbye to coats when I left this hell hole. I just flew back last night. I sure don't miss this winter shit. And I hate hospitals. They make my nerves bad. You wanna grab a drink with me?"

"I don't really drink. Thanks."

You could see our conversation in the February air. Our frozen breath like comic book word bubbles hanging in front of our faces.

"Come on now. Can't trust a man that doesn't drink. I forget who said that but it was somebody famous, I think."

"It's not even 8 AM."

"It's not even 7 AM from where I'm comin' from. What does that matter?"

"I was just heading home, actually. And I'm not really in the mood."

"Well, let me walk with ya, at least. I don't know anyone around here anymore."

People like this have to be told to leave. They'll hang around all night at the store playing dollar scratch-off tickets and telling stories they've told so many times they don't even remember what is true and what is a lie. They don't really care if you're listening or not. They speak just to hear their own voice. My grandfather used to do the same thing. My mom told me it was so he didn't have to think. As long as he kept talking his mind stayed quiet.

"I'm heading back towards downtown if you want to walk with me. I'll show you where the bar is."

"I knew I liked you. Do you have a cigarette I can bum? Did I already ask you that?"

"I don't smoke."

"We can stop and get some on the way."

We head out, side by side.

"So, where are you from?"

"Texas. It was 75 degrees when I left yesterday. Now here I am freezing my nuts off back in the old hometown."

"What brought you back here?"

"My kid got hit by a car yesterday. Her mom called and told me I needed to be here. By the time I got to the hospital everyone had left."

"A little girl?"

"Yeah, why?"

"That's who I was there to see."

"Who the fuck are you? Are you Tammy's brother?"

"I don't know who Tammy is. I was there when the girl got hit yesterday. I was at the hospital to check on her."

"You sure you aren't Tammy's brother? You kinda look like him? If you're lying to me..."

"I don't know who Tammy is," I interrupted.

"Alright, alright. Sorry, kid. I was just making sure. I didn't fly all the way up here to get my ass kicked is all. Just looking out for myself, ya know? A guy's gotta keep a head on his shoulders when he's travelin'."

He sends two sad punches through the space in front of him and smiles a wild smile back at me. I have nothing to add.

"I think the guy blew through the light when she was crossing the street," I blurt out. Trying to break the awkward silence that had settled in between us.

"Damn. Tammy didn't tell me much on the phone. She just told me I needed to get here. I told her I had shit to do, but she said she'd buy the ticket and I could stay with her while I'm here. Thought it might be good to see her."

"I'm so sorry."

"Shit. It's alright. I didn't really know her."

"Your daughter?"

"I talked to her on the phone a few times. Me and her mom met here in town. We moved down to Texas together to get away from our pain in the ass families. She got pregnant and all of a sudden decides she wants to be closer to the family we had just moved away from. I told her I wasn't going to stop her. So she left. I haven't seen her since."

"You didn't want to go with her?"

"Kids happen. Not my fault. I wasn't throwing my life down the drain because she missed her family. I had a job. Shit going on. I'd fucked around long enough in this place. I wasn't coming back."

This was how he spoke. This is how they speak. There's their life and then there's everyone else that revolves around them. He didn't seem to feel anything about his dead daughter aside from the inconvenience the situation caused him. He treated her like she was a stranger and wasn't embarrassed at all. It would be jarring if these weren't almost exact quotes from my grandfather.

"What was your daughter's name?"

"Kaitlyn. But she used her mother's last name. Kaitlyn Dylan. I don't know why she didn't use my last name."

"Probably because you weren't around."

"Doesn't matter if I was there or not. I was still her daddy. She still had my blood in her veins. She should've had my last name. Guess it doesn't matter now."

"I guess it doesn't," I snarled back to him. I turned my head and spit into the street.

We walked down Hospital Hill making our way into downtown together. Him blowing on his hands and talking fast about anything that popped into his head. Commenting on how much the town had changed since he left. I was still processing the situation and offered up only the occasional "yeah" and "sure" to his constant rambling. We were still a few blocks away from my street, but I had had enough of him and decided to turn off and take the long way home.

"I'm turning off here. The bar you're looking for will be just up a couple blocks and make a right. The Angry Steer."

"You sure you don't want a drink? First one's on you. Just kidding. Come on. Just one to get straightened out. Before I go face the shitstorm."

"No thanks. I've been at work all night. I'm heading home. Good luck."

I didn't mean the good luck bit. It just came out.

"Hey, what's your name?" he yelled after me.

"Henry," I shouted back while continuing to walk away.

"Henry, I'm Rick. Nice to meet ya. I'll see ya around." He was shouting now as I moved further down the sidewalk and away from him. I picked up my pace wanting nothing, but more distance between he and I.

I was feeling disgusted and not as surprised as I should have been. I wish people would quit meeting my lowest expectations. Myself included.

I had never met this Tammy, but I hoped she was a better human and parent than Rick. Hearing Rick speak had disturbed me. To hear someone speak of their dead child that way was a lot to handle. I always wish I could be more aggressive towards people like Rick. Not let them bully me around. I can never think of what to do or say in the moment. It's only after the moment has passed that I can ever think of the right thing to say. Even something as small as "Leave me alone," or "I think you're a scumbag." But these words never come. Not until it's too late and I'm left to feel childish and weak for not standing up for myself.

Between the long walk to the hospital and learning of the girl's death and having to speak to Rick, I was now wide awake and sweating underneath my jacket. I unzipped it and picked up my pace now, heading toward the west side of Brooksville. I had no destination and nowhere to be. The cold sweat felt good and my lungs began to adjust to the cold. Being home alone sounded terrifying. I was angry and disappointed with myself and with the world around me. I pointed my body in the direction of the graveyard and just kept walking.

Chapter 39

The next shift at work, I watched the paper delivery guy come in the door and do his normal routine. I wasn't in such a rush now. I knew all I really needed to know. I said hello and returned to my mop making small circles counterclockwise on the white tile floor. I watched my reflection show itself in the bucket then disappear underneath the mop head as I dipped it slowly back into the murky water. I appeared and disappeared 168 times before the floor was clean and ready for the next morning's customers to arrive. Once finished, I walked the bucket to the broom closet and poured the water and all of those reflections down into the drain built into the floor. I dried my hands on my pants and walked to the donut display and reached into the back of the case for a fresh glazed. I grabbed a paper from the rack and took a seat behind the counter.

She was nine years old. Only three blocks from home when she was killed. It was all there in the paper the next morning.

Survived by her mother, Tammy Dylan, and her father, Rick Baker. In lieu of flowers, the family requests donations to help cover the cost of the funeral. A fundraising banquet will be held at the V.F.W. this Saturday from 12 to 7 pm.

These fundraising banquets happened almost every weekend. Someone scraping up money to bury someone they loved or try and make the smallest dent in a stack of medical bills that will never go away. The fold-out tables and single-use tablecloths. Covered dishes and plastic utensils. Family members putting on brave faces around their friends as someone strums an acoustic guitar in the back corner. Rallying around the broken and unfortunate. Some call it community, and in an earlier time maybe it was. But we're too far along now. Some people have private jets and vacation homes. Others have to beg their friends for money to bury their children.

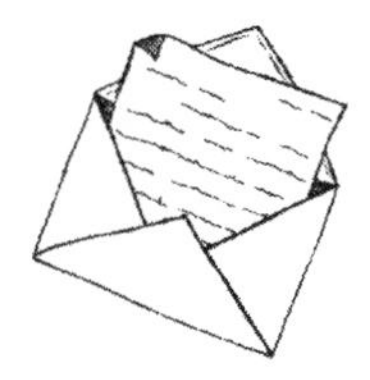

Dear Josh,

There's been a lot going on since we last spoke. Long story short, I saw a little girl get hit by a car downtown and she died. It's been a lot to process and I haven't been able to get myself to even write those words until now. I haven't been sleeping so well since it happened so I've been walking and thinking a lot. Trying to sort my thoughts out and make sense of it all.

I keep seeing the accident over and over in my head. Everytime I lay down to sleep, I relive it. I did everything wrong in the moment. I picked her up and I know I shouldn't have. I don't know if that killed her but I know it didn't help. I ran into her dad at the hospital and he about made me sick.

I haven't heard from you and wanted to let you know where my head's at right now. Any advice is welcome. I'm all ears right now.

Your friend,
Henry

Chapter 40

It's 58 degrees on the first day of March. The sun is just starting to set when I reach the top of the jewelry store on Main Street. It's the highest building in town. The rusty ladder rungs bite into my hands. It feels good to be outside and to feel the sun on my skin. The free movement from the lack of a winter coat feels like a new lease on life. There's a rush that comes with winter beginning to break in cold-weather places. A collective sigh of relief from the entire town.

Empty 40-oz. bottles, burnt-up plastic-tipped cigars and cigarette butts, and the occasional hypodermic needle are scattered about the pebble-covered roof. I watch my step on my way over to the ledge that faces to the south. I stand with my toes hanging out over the ledge looking at the downtown below me, envisioning myself falling through the air and landing in the street. I know it's morbid but I wonder who would find my body and who would come to my funeral. I think of Kaitlyn Dylan and what a human life is really worth. It's all I've been able to think of for some many weeks now. I know it's not healthy, but I can't seem to stop.

To most, she was just a dead kid lying in the middle of the street in some trash town in Ohio. The waste product of a couple of emotionally unstable kids who had sex in a trailer one summer afternoon, left to be carted off and thrown into a hole in the ground. All the pain. The everyday struggle just to exist. For what?

The desperation and hopelessness of these rural slums is a new reality for these areas. The poverty that once mostly affected only urban areas and minorities has found its way into America's heartland and everyone wants to act surprised. They never thought it would affect THEM, of course.

My thoughts race in and out of reality. There's my body laying on the ground below. There's me in the city with friends that talk about politics and have gone to college. We work in bars and restaurants and complain about the customers. I say intelligent things about world leaders and the devastating effects of capitalism. There's me living with my mother in her small apartment here in Brooksville at 40 years old and asking her for money. I watch as the cars drive by and the people down on the sidewalk are walking around in t-shirts. I stand up here and watch the sun set, the fading light highlighting everything in pink as it slowly disappears below the horizon. I look down at the muddy front yards that dot the west end of town. On the wind, I hear the sound of desperate barking dogs and their even louder owners barking right back. The Angry Steer is behind me, just over my right shoulder in fact. I see Kaitlyn dead in the street. Kevin with his deflated head lying on the sidewalk. A car revs its engine down below and shakes me from my daze.

Winter is almost over.

Chapter 41

"Hey, Henry."

"Hey, Mr. Clark. I just mopped, watch your step."

"You have a minute to talk?"

"Yeah. Let me put the mop away. Everything ok?"

"I got a call from Mel and she thought maybe I should come in and check on you is all. I heard about the accident. She mentioned that you were there. That's a lot for a person to handle on their own. I thought maybe you'd want to talk. "

The simple act of someone asking me about the accident opens a flood gate. Before I can even process what he has asked me the words come tumbling from my mouth.

"I hear her voice. And I was unfortunate enough to meet her dad at the hospital and he didn't care if she was dead or alive. And I want to be sad, but there's a big part of me that tells me she's better off than she was or would have been in the long run. And that's a terrible way to think but I fear it might be true."

"Now, that's alright, Henry. There's never a right or wrong way to feel about these kinds of things. It's complicated."

"I keep feeling her weight in my arms. How it changed between the time that I picked her up and the time the ambulance showed up. And everything that I didn't do to help her. It's been all I can think about since it happened."

"Slow down, Henry. Take a minute and breathe."

Mr. Clark turns around and locks the door behind him. He comes behind the counter and gets the CLOSED sign we keep around in case of emergencies. He takes the sign and hangs it up, pressing the rarely used suction cup on the front door. He tugs on the handle to make sure the door was locked.

"Come back in the office with me, Henry. Lets' sit and talk a bit."

I follow Mr. Clark into the back office. There is a small wooden desk covered in receipts and other paperwork. Underneath the desk is a 2-foot-by-2-foot metal safe where the bank deposits are kept. Only Mr. Clark and Mel know the combination. He pulls the swivel chair out from the desk, picks up some paperwork from it, and places it on the already crowded desktop. He slides the chair over to me and then reaches up and grabs an empty red milk crate from the corner to sit on. He pulls at the knees of his khaki pants and groans a bit as he eases himself down onto the crate. I notice how clean his leather penny loafers are. They look soft, like the gloves I took from the lost-and-found box. I suddenly realize the gloves were probably Mr. Clark's. That he might have put them in there for me.

"So Henry, listen. It's alright. Sometimes it's important to have someone to bounce all of these thoughts off of so you don't have to keep them all in your head. It's too much for one person to hold. I understand the hurt and anger. I've been through it. When my wife died it took me months to even say it out loud. Even to myself. I still have trouble saying her name."

He pauses, I guess to see if I need to say anything. When I don't, he starts talking again.

"You know, it still jars my heart when I hear someone else say her name. When I finally started talking about it, I must have went on for an hour before I stopped. And when I did finally stop, I was curled up in a ball on my sister's couch. That was the first time since she had died that I felt human. That what happened felt real. It felt terrible, of course, but at least finally, it was real. For a long time, the worst part of it all was waking up every day and having to relive it. Having to go back and remind yourself that it isn't a dream. That that person is really gone and you will never get to see them again. And then having to start the healing process all over again."

He stops again, and I start up.

"I feel selfish. I didn't even know her. What right do I have to include myself in the pain? I can't even imagine what her mother is feeling right now."

"We all have a right to our own feelings, Henry. That's not being selfish, it's just being aware. It's what makes us human."

"I don't think I like being aware. Or human."

Mr. Clark laughs softly.

"I've thought the same thing at different times in my life, Henry. How much easier it would be to just shuffle through life without all of the suffering and overthinking. The problem is that we're all already here. And there's only one way out. Some days I still wake up and wonder what I'm still doing here. Kicking around, killing time. What time is it now?"

He checks his wristwatch. It's clean gold with a dark brown leather band. Those were definitely Mr. Clark's gloves.

"It's 5:43 in the morning and here I am. I usually fall asleep around 9 at night in my recliner at home watching TV. Sometimes I wake up and go to bed and sometimes I just stay there. The bed still feels so empty without my wife there. What's the point?"

"I don't know, sir. I can't even imagine a loss like that."

"I don't know either, Henry. I'm sorry. I guess I didn't really have a point. Mel had called and seemed concerned about you and that's pretty out of character for her so I thought I should come down."

"I really appreciate it, sir. I really do. I don't have a lot of people to talk to."

"Me either, Henry. Maybe that's a good place for us both to start."

Mr. Clark put his hands on his knees to help himself up. I could heard his knees creak as he stood.

"We're all just getting through this stuff, doing the best we can, Henry. And it's ok to not be ok. I think that's the point I was trying to make. And you're doing a good job here."

"Thank you, Mr. Clark."

I stand up from the swivel chair and extend my hand out to him. He meets my hand with his and shakes my it firmly for a moment before pulling me in closer to him and wrapping his other arm around me in a hug. I hug him back and we stand there for just a moment being human together. We both pull away at the same time and I can see his eyes are on the verge of tears.

"I should get back to the floors, sir," I say.

"Of course, Henry. Of course."

I walk out of the office feeling a little more human than when I walked in.

I am back to mopping the floor when Mr. Clark walks out of the back room with the small, blue bank bag with the daily deposits inside.

"Take care of yourself, Henry," he shouts over to me on his way to the door.

He un-sticks the CLOSED sign from the door and tosses it on the counter before unlatching the lock.

“You too, Mr. Clark,” I say.

The smell of pine cleaner fills the air as I work my way to the back corner of the store. I slosh the mop in the yellow bucket and then wring the mop head out in the connected wringer, watching the water go from clear to brown and then to black by the time I’m done. I feel a golf ball of anxiety forming in my chest and my eyes blur for just a moment. I stand up straight and close my eyes and take a deep breath while using the mop handle to steady myself. I make a promise to no one in particular that I am ok.

Chapter 42

Josh comes to visit:

“This is your place, huh?”

“This is it. Sorry about the mess. If I had known you were coming I would have cleaned up.”

“You live like a serial killer, Henry.”

Josh was never one to hold his tongue.

“Thanks. I don’t spend a lot of time here. I haven’t had a chance or much reason to really decorate.”

“How long have you lived here now?”

“Three years, about. I don’t have a lot of visitors.”

“Some furniture, maybe. A chair at least?”

“You’re the second person other than me to be inside here. I don’t have a lot of use for a chair. Or a table. I have a couple of milk crates around that I took from work. They’re multi-functional. You just have to use a little imagination.”

I hear myself being defensive when I know I shouldn’t be. Josh is only saying out loud what I already know to be true. I just choose not to think about it.

“I’m imagining you hanging in your closet at the moment. Geezus, Henry. And there’s no food here, what do you eat?”

“I usually just eat something at work. Or bring something from work home. I hate going to the grocery store. You never know who you’re going to run into and you’re definitely going to run into someone. It makes me too nervous.”

“We need to get you a cat. You’re way too close to the edge to be living like this. You have to give yourself a reason to wake up and come home. A fish. Something.”

“I have a hard enough time taking care of myself. I’m not trying to add any responsibilities to my life at the moment. And you know I can’t stand pets. I’m not looking to purchase a responsibility that I’m going to have to watch die.”

“It’s not a responsibility as much as it’s something to do. Can I open the blinds at least?”

“Yeah, yeah. Sorry. I sleep during the day so I usually just keep them closed.”

“How’s your mom?”

“She’s good. As good as she gets. Working at some restaurant. I don’t know how the place even stays in business. The only people that go there are the old folks in town and they don’t tip. And they only pay her two bucks an hour.”

“Is that legal?”

“That’s what I asked. I guess because she gets tips they can pay less than minimum wage. How is anyone supposed to live off of that? I barely get by on what I make. I don’t know how she does it.”

"We all make do. Somehow. People can get used to anything. Does she know that there's more out there? That she can leave?"

"I've brought it up before and she always gives me the same blank look. It used to really piss me off until I got older and started understanding that she honestly had no idea where she would go or that she was even able to go. I think her life was so hard when she was young that it took all of her energy just to escape her family situation. Once she got through that she didn't have the energy to think about going any further. You know she's never owned a car? I don't know that she's ever been out of Ohio."

"Neither have you."

"At least I've thought about leaving. I mean, I know I need to leave. That's something at least. I need to save some money to get me through the first few months. If I left and then had to come back I would just climb right back up on top of the jewelry store and jump."

"You know the jewelry store is only four stories, right? You might break a bone or two, but the fall isn't going to kill you."

"It's the tallest building in town."

"You know what, you have to come to the city, if only to find a proper building to jump off. Come on, let's get the fuck out of here. I can't stay in this apartment another minute."

When I woke up to someone knocking, I assumed it was the mail person or my landlady. Despite it being four o'clock in the afternoon, I was groggy and pissed off when I ripped open the front door. But there was Josh. I hadn't seen him in so long I almost didn't recognize him at first. He didn't look like a kid from Brooksville now. He had a haircut, a real one. Not one you do in the mirror by yourself. And he was wearing clothes that actually fit him. Not second-hand hand-me-downs. He kept catching me staring at him as I was hurrying to get dressed. Every minute he spent in my apartment felt like an eternity. I was embarrassed for myself. I wanted out of there as badly as he did.

"So what should we get into?" Josh asked.

"The coffee shop closes at 5 and it's 4:38 now. So that's out. We could go eat somewhere? We could go and check if my mom's working?"

"I just ate a little bit ago. How about a drink?"

"Yeah, sure. I'm off tonight. Are you drinking now?" I regret asking this as soon as it leaves my mouth. I sound like a worried mother questioning her child. I'm relieved when he doesn't call me on it.

"Here and there. It's more for something to do. After spending 18 years in Brooksville I really appreciate having places to go after five in the afternoon that I don't have to constantly be looking over my shoulder or worried someone's going to kick the shit out of me because of my last name. I like leaving my windows open and hearing the sounds of a city. I got my fill of quiet country nights when I was here. I find city noise inspiring."

"Well, you know where you are. I'll let you pick the place. Let's see. Sports bar? Townie bar? That terrifying place with the apartments upstairs? The joint by the railroad tracks?"

"I don't feel like dying at the moment, so we'll start at the sports bar and go from there."

I started to feel better as soon as I locked the door of my apartment. I felt the anxiousness in my chest start to dissipate and breathing became easier. We started down the sidewalk, heading east towards town. We stopped on the bridge that runs over the trickle of a river that snakes it's way southeast through town. We both picked up some small rocks out of the street and started throwing them as far as we could out into the water. A pastime we'd enjoyed as kids. We would throw the rocks and watch the ripples move out from their landing spot and then disappear. I still found it surprisingly therapeutic.

We both threw in silence, letting things be quiet and easy. For a few moments at least. Josh spoke first.

"It's weird being back here. It seems like a different lifetime ago that I lived here. Like it was a different person that lived here. Me, but not me."

"How does that feel?"

"Good. But disorienting. I feel good about leaving. And I don't mean that in a bad way. I'm not here to shit on you or even the town, really. I just feel different. I don't feel connected to this place anymore."

"How's the city different? I mean, I'm sure that it is. But how is it different?"

"People don't know who I am there. Not only that, they don't care who I am. I know wherever we go right now I'm going to know someone and they're going to know me. At least what they knew of me when I was a kid. All the preconceived notions that follow you around in these small towns. Something you did when you were fourteen can define you until the day you die in a place this small. In the city I'm no one. Just another person caught up in the hustle. I find that comforting."

"Doesn't it get lonely?"

"Of course it does. But I was lonely here. Humans are lonely by nature. There's no escaping that. It's learning how to be alone that's important. You can learn a lot about yourself by spending time alone. Have you dug into the new *Memory Currency*?"

"I haven't got the new one yet. But I've spent quite a bit a time with last month's. And I told you I went back and read some of the first issues you and I bought together. From what I can tell the reader is living inside of the writer's head. The changing of artists on different pages and jumping from space to earth and back to space. The whole premise is that you are inside of the writer's head and you are seeing inside of his ideas while he's writing it. It's almost interactive. And it makes way more sense once you realize it's not supposed to make sense. It's not a linear story. It's just a really far-out idea this guy was going for."

"Wow. I had no clue. So what about this Captain Jane business then?"

"Ok. Stick with me here. And keep in mind I'm making this up and have no idea if this is right. But I think Captain Jane is the personification of an idea. Every time she shows up a new idea is introduced. Whether it's a changing of landscape or introducing a new character. It's a visual for the reader to show the writer having an idea. And the different drawings of Captain Jane represent what kind of an idea it is. If it's an idea for a conversation, it's her with green hair and a more crude line drawing. When she's representing a new character she's drawn perfectly with the fiery red hair just like in the first issues."

Josh starts to laugh and puts a hand on my shoulder.

"You have way too much time on your hands. Let's get a drink before we dive any deeper into Captain Jane."

Chapter 43

Josh and Henry hit the town:

I haven't been to this place in years. It sold itself as a sports bar and pizza place. What it really is an extension of the boys locker room in high school. They even have pictures of the current high school sports teams on the wall. The kids from the pictures bring your pizza to your table and the star quarterbacks from years past tend the bar. The clientele seemed to be all the people from high school that didn't get enough the first time around.

"What are you having, Henry?"

"This place gives me the creeps."

"That's why we're here. We're exploring your environment. What'll it be?"

"A beer, I guess."

Josh calls for the bartender. The kid's a bit younger than us but looks familiar. There are only about eight last names in the entire town. Your last name in a small town is like your business card. All of your information is right there for everyone to see. Once someone knows your last name they know what part of town you live in, what your parents do or don't do, about how much money you make. What your siblings have done or not done. All out there on the table for everyone to see. If your parent was a fuck-up drunk, you're a fuck-up drunk. From the time you walk into elementary school the teachers know exactly who you are and what they should expect from you.

"Two Budweisers," Josh yells over to the bartender holding two fingers in the air.

"Your rationale for Budweiser is?"

"To not draw attention to ourselves. What's with the shrines to these little kids on the walls? They're children. This should be illegal."

"That seventh-grade swim team over the bar is terrifying. Their eyes follow you."

"We'll have one beer here and then move on."

We both start to settle down from the excitement of seeing one another. Falling quickly back into old conversations and inside jokes. We talk politics. Local and national. We talk about Brooksville's fraud of a mayor and about the game show host who has just been elected president. We both agree the situation is dire, as per usual. For a moment, I think about the two old guys at the coffee shop in their overalls and about Josh and I sitting here having our same old conversations. I laugh at the thought but keep it to myself. It feels good to not be alone. To not hesitate with my words. We notice some of our old gym teachers, now with red noses, drinking beer from large frosted mugs in the corner. They're laughing loudly and smacking the table with their palms. Swatting each other's backs. One of them finishes a story he's telling, saying "What a faggot," loud enough for us to hear. The whole group of them cackles in response. It's only a matter of minutes before they start arm-wrestling. Josh and I share a quick glance that says it's time for us to leave.

We pay for our drinks and head for the front door. One of the gym teachers yells something at us as the door is closing, but we're too far out of earshot to make out what it is. We both decide it's best to keep moving.

"Ok. One more stop, then I have to split."

"You're leaving tonight?"

"Yeah. I have to get back to work tomorrow. I just came to check in on you after your last letter. I could tell you were having a hard time."

"I really appreciate that."

"I know you do, Henry."

I'm thankful for how we are able to fall right back into the rhythm of our friendship. The easy conversation. The way we speak honestly to each other, without worrying about motives. Even after so much time had passed.

"Well, the choices are train tracks, apartment bar, or townie?"

Josh smiles.

"Into the devil's den we go. Remind you where you come from."

He says the last in his finest rural American drawl. Most people in town spoke with some kind of southern drawl. Even though it's northern Ohio. I asked my mom once why that was and she told me "that's just how we speak," but I don't talk like that and I grew up here. Most of the kids I went to school with had different levels of this rural slur. It seemed to stem more from a lack of money than anything to do with location.

I take a loud dramatic breath and follow Josh's lead.

When we arrive, I grab the handle and pull back the heavy, solid wood door open and motion with my hand for Josh to walk into the Angry Steer first. The old heads at the bar all turn our way. Old men in overalls and mesh-back hats with seed and tractor brand names and logos. The younger people in the back room are yelling and playing pool. We find two open stools at the far end of the bar.

"Henry, I'm gonna hit the bathroom. Order me whatever you're having."

Steve emerges from the back room, balancing a stack of pint glasses in one hand and a beer bottle in the other.

"Hey, Steve!"

"Henry! What brings you around?"

"You said to come in and have a drink sometime. So, here I am."

"Well alright. What'll it be then?"

"Two Budweisers, I guess. And two shots of tequila."

"Alright. Lime or salt with that tequila?"

"Up. Is that right? That means no lime or salt, right?"

"It sure does. Two Buds and two tequilas coming right up. What's the celebration?"

"Existence."

The other side of this place where the pool tables are used to be a barbershop. My mom took me there a couple of times when I was a kid. I forget the old guy's name, but I remember he was always pissed off when we came in. Like you were bothering him. He was always telling me to sit still and I would swear that I was. Not that it mattered. He only knew the single haircut he had learned in the military and that's what everyone got. The only difference was how many times he nicked your ears with the shears while his arthritic hand shook.

I glance up to the TV behind the bar and there's a college basketball game playing on the screen. I can't tell which team is which but I stare at the screen anyway. The sound is turned down but I find myself fixated on the squeaking of shoes against hardwood that I know I would hear if the sound was up. I get startled back to reality when Steve shows up with the drinks.

"Sorry I can't stick around, Henry. Tomorrow's delivery day and I have to be back here at 6 AM to open up. I told Jesse to put another round on the house for ya."

Steve sets the drinks down in front of me and double taps his right hand on the bar. I don't know what this means, but I assume it's a kind of bar talk or code for something. I thank Steve for the drinks and promise to stop in again when he has more time. He thanks me for coming in and tells me to not be a stranger. He tosses his bar rag back by the liquor bottles and grabs his keys from a bowl next to the cash register and heads for the back door. He pauses on his way out, shouts over to me, and asks if I'm alright. I yell back that I've never felt better. He raises his keys in the air in his right hand and heads out the door.

Josh appears at my side.

"It's like a really bad class reunion back there."

"Shit. You can't be sneaking up on people in a place like this."

"Sorry. I forgot where I was. Anybody bother ya while I was gone?"

"Nah. Steve just left. He said he wished he could stay, but he has to be back here at 6AM. He bought us these and another round if we want it."

"I always did like that guy."

"To Steve."

"To Steve."

I've never had tequila before and it tastes like fire. Now I know what the salt and lime are for. Josh and I both cough and my eyes start to water. I am still convincing my body everything is alright when I see Kaitlyn's dad, Rick, stumble in from the back room.

"Shit," I say out loud to myself.

"You alright?" Josh asks.

"It's the little girl's dad."

Rick sees us and looks genuinely excited to see me.

"Hey, hey! Look who it is! Henry, right?"

He is still wearing the same clothes he was wearing at the hospital. He reeks of booze and he's slurring his words. My mind tries to figure out what it's supposed to do with the tequila.

"I thought you'd be back in Texas by now," I say.

"Well, me and Tammy have been getting along pretty well. Thought I'd stay here for a bit. She's pretty broken up about everything and I wanna be here for her. Help her through, ya know?"

"Such a gentleman all of a sudden."

I surprise myself with this answer. I like the confidence the tequila is giving me.

"I wanted to talk to you, Henry. Tammy and I got a lawyer and she seems to think we have a pretty good case against the kid who hit our little Kaitlyn."

I am just starting to open my mouth when Josh speaks up.

"What the fuck is wrong with you, man?"

"What do ya mean? Just trying to get justice for my little girl."

"You didn't even know her," I spit.

"Now that's my little girl you're talking about. I may not have been any father of the year, but it was my blood running through her veins."

Josh stands up and moves around me, closer to Rick.

"Fuck your scummy blood and fuck you."

Josh is now inches from Rick's face. I have never seen Josh this mad.

I see the punch coming in slow motion. The years of being fucked up have slowed Rick's reaction time. I step aside, and watch as a beer bottle explodes on Rick's face. His nose opens up like a fountain and he stumbles back with his hands on his face, screaming.

"Run!" Josh yells.

I reach into my pocket and toss a $10 dollar bill onto the bar and follow Josh out the front door. We run for blocks, stopping on the street around the corner from my apartment. We are both doubled over with our hands on our knees panting, trying to catch our breath.

"Geezus Christ!" I yell. I'm not sure if it is out of anger, fear, or maybe both.

"Sorry. It just kind of happened," Josh says.

"We should get inside. Before anyone comes looking for us."

"There's nobody coming, Henry. Not for us and not for that guy. That kind of stuff happens in there every day. He'll get cleaned up in the bathroom and keep drinking and by tomorrow he'll forget what even happened. Don't sweat it. I have to get going though. My bus leaves in an hour."

"You're going? Now?"

"I have to work tomorrow. I just came to check on you."

We stand there on the sidewalk, still catching our breath. Just as I begin to breathe normally, I start laughing. The fit hits Josh and he starts laughing too. We stand there on the sidewalk like that for a while before the laughter finally subsides and we say our goodbyes. We head off in different directions but I swear I can hear Josh still laughing in my head, even after he's gone.

I walk slowly around the corner to my place. Enjoying the lightheadedness of the alcohol, the adrenaline of the fight still present even as it fades. I can't remember the last time I had laughed like that. The muscles in my face hurt from smiling. I unlock the door to my apartment and for probably the first time ever, I feel happy to be home. I go into the kitchen and get the trash can, and walk through the apartment cleaning up the old plastic Coke bottles, the donut boxes, the gas-station food wrappers. I fill two full-size trash bags by the time I am finished. I walk outside and toss them into the dumpster behind the apartment building.

Chapter 44

I walk back inside and lock the door behind me. I go to my bedroom, strip down to my boxers and a t-shirt, and flop down on the futon mattress. I pick up the copy of *Memory Currency* laying on the floor beside me. I try to focus on the first few pages, but my eyes are still a little blurry from the alcohol and running.

I put the comic back down on the floor next to my bed and close my eyes. I lay there replaying everything over and over in my head. I am trying to decide if I should feel guilty about how good I feel when I finally drift off to sleep.

That night I dream of being trapped inside a body bag.

An ambulance shows up to my apartment and the cops and EMTs just let themselves in. I am laying in bed when they find me. I try to tell them that I am not dead but they can't hear me. I try to punch and kick them—anything to make them realize that I am not dead—but nothing works. I can't convince my arms or legs to move. I scream but no one hears me. I watch as the zipper of the body bag slides past my face and the world goes black. I hear one of the EMTs telling a joke about a horse and a bartender while they carry me out the front door of my apartment and toss my body in the ambulance. I am still screaming as they close the doors. They stop at a Chinese restaurant on their way to the morgue.

For some strange dream reason, I can hear their conversation inside the restaurant through the darkness. They don't discuss me at all. They laugh at each other's fortunes. From inside the bag, I get a vision of my mother answering the door at her apartment. It's a cop who picks her up and takes over to the morgue to identify my body. Finally, the zipper slides back and the light floods in and I see my mother's face as she realizes it really is me lying there. She starts to cry and I feel so sorry for her. I'm still screaming as they zip the bag back up.

Chapter 45

"WQRC: THE HITS YOU MISS! I'm Randy Ranger filling in for Daisy D. this morning. It's 8:03 and I'm here with your news and classic oldies until noon .... You'll want to stay clear of Clinton Street today. There's been a water main break and it's going to be a flooded mess over there until crews can get it all cleaned up .... The Brooksville Marching Band is in Massillon today fighting for a chance to head to the state Division 4 championship .... Molly Swinski is turning 92 years young today out at Brooksville Nursing and Aging Center. Maybe stop by and wish Molly a happy birthday .... That's it for now. Coming up is the classic hit 'Lollipop' by the Chordettes right after these messages from our lovely sponsors!"

***

I reach over and swat at the alarm clock, missing twice before finally reaching over and ripping the plug from the wall. There have to be more songs recorded in the 50s and 60s than goddamned "*Lollipop.*"

I lay in bed trying to focus as the details from last night start coming back. I didn't have that much to drink, but a shot and a couple beers is 100 percent more than I am accustomed to. My stomach squirms and my head feels hollow. I stare at the ceiling for as long as I can until the urge to pee forces me up and into the bathroom to start my day.

One upside of my job is that a lot of the expired or damaged goods are free for the taking. I try not to take too much advantage of it, but when a case of some new coffee drink doesn't sell and it not worth shipping back, it comes home with me.

I open one up and the smell that comes from the bottle is enough to push me over the edge. I vomit all over the kitchen floor. There was definitely some sort of milk product in there with the coffee that was way past its prime. I make my way to the sink and gag and heave for a while. I turn on the faucet and let it run. From the looks of the floor, what came up is mostly stomach acid. I pour the bottle down the drain while my stomach muscles continue contracting and convulsing. I lay my hot cheek on the cool countertop as the sound of the running faucet soothes my brain. As I regain composure I can't help but laugh at myself. I wonder how Rick with the busted face is feeling today. I know it has to be worse than this.

I clean up the kitchen and force myself into the shower. I stand there letting the warm water run over my head for a good ten minutes. When the water stops getting hot, I frantically wash my body and hair before it goes completely cold. I take my time getting ready for the day. I plug my alarm clock radio back into the wall and reset the time. I turn it up as loud as it will go so that I can hear it throughout the apartment. Josh opened the curtains yesterday and the sun is shining into the living room. I crack a couple of windows to let some fresh air in. It's sunny and cool outside, but the brutal winter chill is gone.

I think about buying a chair.

I decide to go see my mom.

"Henry!"

"Hey Mom."

"You're up awfully early this morning."

"I had some things I wanted to do today. Where's your section?"

"The four tables back in the corner. Sally's son is working today and she always gives him the only decent section in the place. Sticks me with the dark corner no one wants to sit in."

I walk back to a dark corner booth. The two tables next to it are empty and the booth in front of me is taken by Ray. Everyone in town knows Ray and mostly leaves him alone. He doesn't bother anyone and they don't bother him. He doesn't talk much and when he does you can't understand him. He was in a car accident when he was a teenager and never really mentally recovered. Now he just wanders through town, collecting free coffee and occasional spare change. He's lived in one of the apartments above the Angry

Steer for as long as I've known him. I wave hello and he stares blankly back at me. Classic Ray.

"So what'll it be today?" My mom asks.

"Two pancakes, bacon, and... is the pie any good?"

"It's been sitting in that glass case since last weekend."

"Not the pie then."

"You want anything to drink besides water? Chocolate milk, maybe?"

"That sounds perfect. Thanks Mom."

"Let me get this into the kitchen and I'll come sit with you."

As my mom walks away she asks Ray if he's alright. He holds up his coffee cup in response. She tells him she'll be right back with a warm-up.

I watch her make her way back to the kitchen through the set of swinging doors behind the counter. I notice the Scarface poster has been taken down. A minute later she comes back carrying a full coffee pot, stopping to fill Ray's coffee cup on her way back to me.

She sets the coffee pot down on the counter and then comes back over to where I'm sitting. She eases herself down in the booth across from me with an audible "oaf."

"What's on your mind, kiddo?"

"Did you hear about that accident?" I ask.

"Oh, I did. It just broke my heart. I heard she was only nine years old."

"I was there."

"What do you mean?"

"I was there. I saw it happen. I held her. I told her that her mom was coming. I sang to her. She was bleeding pretty bad and I didn't know what to do. It was so cold out. I couldn't just let her lay there."

"Oh, Henry."

"And I think she died. While I was holding her. She got quiet and then she got real heavy."

My mom has her hands over her mouth and I can see she's starting to cry. And that makes me start to cry. Suddenly, there's a crashing sound from the kitchen and it startles us both.

"I haven't felt much like talking about it, but I saw Josh last night and we talked. I woke up this morning and realized I wanted to talk to you. It just felt like I needed to."

"You saw Josh last night?"

"Yeah. He came into town to see me."

My mom sits quietly for a moment and then says she'll be right back. A few moments later, she comes back with the food and sets it on the table. Everything smells delicious.

"Are you gonna be ok? I'm gonna see if I can scrounge up a few tables."

"I'm feeling better already."

As a product of TV babysitter generation, I grew up watching commercials that never failed to show me everything I was missing out on. One thing I knew was that if there was enough money for fast food, that meant things were going pretty well for me and my mom. It pisses me off to this day when I hear people complaining about fast food and the quality or taste or how it's filled with sugar. Yes, it is. And yes it is! And someone else is making it for you and if you are complaining about the taste of that stuff, then I don't believe you have ever spent any real time with a little food company called ValuTime.

We lived on ValuTime everything growing up. The company makes everything from sugar to flour to bread, and all of their products are labeled plainly as such. It's unsettling. My theory is that all ValuTime products are actually made of some kind of magical paste that is just pressed into different forms. They even make a cheese that somehow doesn't melt. The thing is, I'm not trying to knock ValuTime because if it wasn't for them we would've gone hungry many nights. At the same time, I'm positive that anyone complaining about a McDonald's cheeseburger hasn't lived for weeks on ValuTime bologna and white bread.

We all have things our brains equate with love. And we do things every single day that are against our better interests in order to chase down that feeling. Some people exercise 12 times a week. Some people wash chocolate bars down with Mountain Dew. Some people stick a needle in their arm. All in an attempt to feel a little less alone.

The pancakes are perfect.

Chapter 46

"WQRC: THE HITS YOU MISS! - Good afternoon Brooksville! You've got Randy Ranger here tuned in on 97.3. As many have you have probably already heard about the tragedy of the accident downtown a few days ago. We've been keeping you up to date as best we can. Kaitlyn Dylan was hit and killed by a car off Main Street. The driver was a 22-year-old male from Attica, Ohio. The police report says the driver went through a red light and hit the girl while she was stepping into the intersection. The driver has been released on bail until his court date next week. Our hearts go out to Kaitlyn and her family. We haven't received word on the funeral or visiting hours, but we will be sure to report them to you as soon as we hear something."

"In more uplifting news, the Brooksville Dog and Cat Rescue is having a fundraiser this weekend out at Rheinmiller Park. The event will take place at the indoor/outdoor picnic bunker next to the pool and playground. Come out and find your new best friend! Our very own Daisy D. from here at WQRC will be spinning your favorite oldies and food will be provided by Pearl's Bar and Grill. We'd love to see you out there. Now let's get back to the music!"

I say it out loud: "Don't do it, Rick."

"Let's kick it off with a little Beach Boys, some fun in the sun ..."

"Thank you."

"Oh wait, I read that wrong. Here's one of my favorites, here's the Chordettes with their 1958 classic, 'Lollipop.'"

"God dammit!"

It's all that I can do to not throw the alarm clock against the wall and smash it to pieces. The anger and sadness are fist-fighting inside of my stomach. Sadness wins as I sit in my room on the futon mattress thinking of that little girl and the accidental nonsense of life. We come and go so quickly. None of it fair. Or thought out. Old people dying hurts, but at least it makes some kind of sense. A child dying is almost too much for my brain to process.

I allow myself to sit and lose my mind for two minutes and sixteen seconds.

Chapter 47

Life takes on the meaning that we give it. There is nothing more than that once it's gone.

Chapter 48

"One coffee, please. Black."

The man working behind the counter of the coffee shop grunts and turns his back to me without saying a word. He picks a cup from the plastic rack by the sink and fills it at the large metal tank that sits on the counter. He proceeds to walk to the far counter and clank the white coffee cup down on the blue tile.

"Dollar eighty-five," he says into the air with no direct aim. Obviously irritated with my presence.

I set three dollars on the front counter and thank him. He says nothing in return. I make the awkward and silent six-step walk over to the far counter where he has set my coffee.

I am walking towards an open chair near the back of the shop by the greeting card racks and knick-knacks with my black coffee in hand when I see Marge sitting in a brown leather recliner on the south side wall. I'm excited and surprised to see her and head over to say hello.

"Marge?"

"Henry!"

"I'm really glad to see you, Marge. How are you?"

"Another day above ground, Henry. Did you meet Hank behind the counter?"

"Lovely fellow."

"Hank's an asshole. His wife owns the place and it drives him crazy that it's successful."

"Isn't that right, Hank?" Marge shouts over in Hank's direction.

Hank's now sitting on a stool behind the cash register, reading the newspaper over the top of a pair of reading glasses. He ignores us both.

"What are you doing right now, Henry?"

"Sitting here with you."

"When's the last time you went bowling?"

"Hmmm, it's probably been close to 20 years."

"Wanna go?"

"Now?"

"Come on. It'll be fun."

She stands up, grabs her purse, and walks over to the far counter. I heard her yell for Hank. She comes back with a to-go cup for my coffee. I am careful in the transfer, not wanting to anger Hank with any kind of mess to clean up.

I follow Marge to her car where it's parked right outside the front door of the coffee shop. It looks to me like a brand new Cadillac. It's red, but not a cheap bright red. Much closer to wine than a crayon. The sun is out and the reflection makes it look like it's made of glass. Marge yells over top of the car from the driver side for me to get in. I hesitate.

"Something wrong?"

"I haven't ridden in a car in a long time. And I've never ridden in a car this nice."

"Shit, Henry. It's just a car. Nothing special. Get in."

I open the door and the smell of leather comes pouring out. I slide carefully into the passenger seat. When I close the door a bell dings and the seat belt automatically slides across my chest. I know this may sound outlandish or even dopey, but I had never seen anything like this before. When else would I have ridden in a Cadillac? Or a even car built in the last ten years?

The dashboard looks like what I imagine an airplane cockpit would look like. The little symbols and gauges and blinking lights resemble a Las Vegas slot machine.

"You ok over there?" Marge asks.

"Yeah. Of course," I say, trying to sound calm despite all of the information my brain is taking in at the moment. My seat is starting to feel warm. I choose to work under the assumption that this is supposed to be happening, a normal thing.

We pull out onto Main Street in a smooth glide. I had almost forgotten what riding in a car had felt like. My heart is beating fast and my palms begin to sweat.

"Do you mind if we listen to some music?" Marge asks.

"Of course not. What did you have in mind?"

"Beethoven's Fifth."

She moves her fingers gently around the steering wheel and the first notes of Beethoven's Fifth come booming from the speakers. It startles me and I'm immediately embarrassed.

"Sorry. I like to listen to it loud. It's so dramatic. Wonderful driving music. It makes me feel like I'm living inside of a movie. Even if

I'm driving to a bowling alley. I'm going to take the long way if you don't mind."

"Not at all."

I settle in and try to relax. The music is beautiful. Everything outside passes by so quickly. I keep thinking about how long it takes me to walk to certain points as we pass them. For example, it's a 25-minute walk from the sports bar, dipping down into the north-side flood land, and then up to the top of Hospital Hill. In the Cadillac, it takes seconds. We pass the hospital and head out beyond the businesses and out onto the county road. It's been years since I'd been this far north. I am surprised to see that the pizza place on the far north end has changed its name from "Mikey's, Home Of The Turnover" to "Fat Boyz." The use of the "z" seems odd to me.

"We'll take the new connector road they just finished out here. I haven't driven on it yet and we're just getting to my favorite part of this piece."

Marge yells to me over the music.

"Ok," I shout back.

I have never actually listened to Beethoven before, but I can't imagine a better way to experience it for the first time than riding in a brand new Cadillac. I think about the fact that people do this type of thing every day and it makes me feel ashamed. I think of my little apartment. My second-hand clothes. That we drove by the restaurant my mom was working at like it wasn't there, like she wasn't there. And how many hours either of us would have to work to ever buy a car like this.

We fly down the county road, passing the farm houses and the old cider mill in a blur. The music continues to go from loud to soft and soft to loud. And Marge is right. I feel like I'm living inside of a movie. Someone should be narrating my thoughts in a booming voice over the top of the things passing before my eyeballs.

"Can I roll the window down?" I call out.

Marge smiles and my window goes down without me cranking on any handles or even pressing a button. The wind whips through the car and I look over to the dashboard to see we are sitting at 73 mph as we tear past the 55 mph speed limit sign. My seat is almost on fire now and the cool air feels good whipping through the car. Marge turns the music up a little more with the push of a button on the steering wheel.

Soon enough, we slam to a halt at a stop sign. Marge looks hurriedly in both directions. Beethoven is pouring over us as we make a right onto the new road in town, "Connector 30." Marge hits the gas and we accelerate in a buttery silence. I can't decide if it feels like melting or floating.

I'm disappointed when after only four miles we pull off Connector 30 and slow to another stop. We are now on the far eastern part of town. Marge brings us back into the city limits at an easy 37 mph. When we pull into the bowling alley parking lot, she turns Beethoven down to a dull roar and finds a spot near the front door. She shuts the car off with the push of a button.

"She runs smooth, huh?" Marge asks.

A smile spreads slowly across my face, like an oil spill.

I nod.

"I do enjoy driving it. And I have never heard Beethoven sound better than inside this car. That was my main selling point."

I haven't been to the bowling alley in years, but when we walk through the doors, the sound of the pins crashing and the smell of stale popcorn makes me feel like I am eight years old again. It's all the same. From the battered swirl-patterned carpet to the old guy behind the counter spraying the shoes with whatever it is they spray rented bowling shoes with. It's the middle of the afternoon so there are only a couple of folks bowling over on the far left lanes. Marge and I walk up to counter together.

"A women's nine for me and, what size shoe are you, Henry?"

"Eleven."

"And an eleven, please."

The man behind the counter finds our sizes and sets two pairs—both red on one side, blue on the other, and tan down the middle with velcro straps—on the counter. He's probably in his late-40s, wearing a white polo shirt with a bowling ball stitched onto the left side of the chest. He's got one of those arm braces that bowlers wear on his right wrist like we have interrupted him in the middle of a game.

"Lane 14," he says waving us off with his braced hand.

We find lane 14 and settle in to change our shoes.

The last time I was here I was eight years old. It was the only time I remember my mom allowing me to be alone with my grandfather. I remember him drinking beer from the clear plastic cups. The smell of his breath each time he bent down to give me the ball. I recall his patience with me, how he taught me to line my feet up with the triangles on the lanes. He was slow and methodical, the cigarette dangling in the corner of his mouth the whole time, wiggling when he spoke.

The smoke burnt my eyes when he stood over me, but I didn't complain. It felt good to be fussed over. I can see now that he was excited to teach me something that he felt he was good at. One of the last things in life he hadn't completely fucked up. When he was bowling, he was still in control. Taking the ball from the return, running the towel over it to wipe the oil from the lanes away. Steadying himself and aligning his feet with the arrows. The deep breath, his practiced four-step approach. With bowling, he knew exactly what he needed to do to succeed. And if he failed, he knew how to adjust for the next ball. It was like meditation for him, with the added bonus that he could drink. The rest of his life was chaos. Chaos that he had created for himself, but chaos nonetheless. I always had fond memories of that day. Years later, it came back to me that he ended up in the bar halfway through our game and never came back. My grandmother had to come and pick me up and take me home.

"Your turn, Henry." Marge says. Shaking me from my own head.

I take the ball from the ball return. I line my left foot up with the arrow that is one left of the middle arrow and focus my eyes on the arrows out on the lane. I focus my eyes on the arrow that lies one to the right of the middle. Breathe. Approach. Lay it down gentle and straight on the lane.

I do all of these things. I release the ball and it feels smooth and natural. I blink and hold my breath before opening my eyes to see the ball fall into the left gutter three quarters of the way down the lane. I hear Marge's laugh come from behind me.

"Throw another one, Henry. And try relaxing this time. This is supposed to be fun."

I laugh when she says this. And she's right. I try and relax and forget all of the tips my grandfather gave me. I throw the ball as hard as I can on the second turn and knock down three pins. It feels good to connect. Marge claps behind me.

"There ya go, kid. Just give 'em hell and forget about it."

"That felt good. Knocking something down." I say excitedly back to her.

"It helps me relax. I like it out here in the afternoon. I like the sounds. And knocking things down does feel pretty good. Let's a little pressure off. That second one had some real nerve in it. You doing ok?"

"I honestly don't know. My friend Josh came into town last week and it was really good to see him, but it also reminded me that I'm not doing anything with myself. And it's starting to take a toll on me."

"May I give you some motherly advice?"

"I wish you were my mother," I joke, saying it without thinking.

"Oh, I would have messed you up beyond repair, Henry. That's a big reason I never had kids in the first place. We're all so full of these emotional issues handed down by our parents and their parents from their parents. We're all wound up in it and we have no idea how to get out of the cycle. Your loneliness is driving you a bit mad, but that's to be expected. You're human. Loneliness drives us all. We are all constantly searching for even the smallest moment of connection to one another. It's why we listen to music and write poetry and pretend to fall in love. That search has driven many people absolutely crazy. And I do not blame them one bit."

"I feel so empty most of the time. Like I'm sleepwalking. But I keep getting older. And the emptiness keeps getting worse and I have no idea how to fill it."

"We're all caught here, Henry. Trying to fill in that emptiness. Some people have children, some people get married, some turn against the world and get angry at it. As much as it's not your fault that you're here, it's nobody else's fault either. It's up to you to find something that fulfills you in a positive way. Anything else will eat at you and turn all of that energy you feel now into a negative bowling ball. Crushing everything that gets in its way. The worst of us comes out when we're not paying attention."

Marge and I laugh and talk through all ten frames. I roll a 64 and Marge rolls a 102. Neither of us feel too bad about our performance, but we decide one game is enough. We place our rented shoes back on the counter to be sprayed and displayed and head back out to her car. It takes a minute for my eyes to adjust to the sun after being inside the dark bowling alley. We take the long way back to the coffee shop and finish Beethoven's Fifth with the windows of the Cadillac open to the world.

Chapter 49

Marge had quickly become someone that I admired. She spoke differently than anyone else I knew. She had gone out into the world and chased her dreams. And she spoke of that wider world in a way that made it seem possible for anyone to enter.

Poverty doesn't allow for the luxury of looking ahead to the future. There's not much time for contemplation. All your time is taken up with the struggle to exist. I had some luxury and privilege, being a white male a generation removed from my mother's chaotic childhood. And I had some time and relative comfort that allowed me to look outside of myself and my situation. My generation knows there is more to this world than just working and dying, but not feeling like you have access to that larger world is a tough non-opioid pill to swallow. But I do not want to let this world turn me cold and angry. I want to be better than what I came from. And I want to let others know they can be better too. Hearing Marge talk inspired me.

When I got home from the bowling alley, I emptied the glass jar of change I call a savings account onto the floor. Mostly pennies, nickels, and dimes, with the occasional quarter. There were even three of those dollar coins that no one uses and I always have to apologize for when I spend them or give them to people as change. I started with the pennies, counting up from there.

I wasn't sure what my next move was, but I knew money always helps.

Chapter 50

The grocery store is the social hub of a small town. The place where plans are made and gossip is passed. I walk through the automatic doors and the familiar smell of refrigeration attacks my senses. I find the customer service desk on the far side of the store, keeping my head down in hopes of dodging anyone I might know. The change jar is tucked under my right arm.

To the right of customer service is the change machine that you can dump all of your change into and for a small fee it counts it up and spits out a paper receipt that you can cash in at the counter.

I started counting my change up at home, but hadn't even finished counting the pennies before I decided I needed to find another way. Counting by hand would've saved me a couple bucks but I decided it was worth the few bucks to save the time. I press the start button and begin pouring my change into the metal basket that tips down and sends the coins into the machine to be counted. It's loud and I'm embarrassed by all of the clicking and clacking of the coins falling. I keep my eyes straight ahead and hope that no one is paying attention to me. The sound is like a poor person siren. I'm surprised there aren't any bells going off to draw even more attention. I breathe a little easier when the counter on the digital screen gets up over $50 dollars. That was my goal. Anything after that is bonus. The coins keep clacking away and I have to keep tipping the tray up to move the change into the belly of the machine. As I get the last of the coins into the machine the metal against metal thunderstorm slows to a trickle.

$87.01!

The machine spits out the receipt. I take it and get in line at the service counter.

There's an old man leaning against the counter scratching lottery tickets. His shoulders are slumped and he's squinting at the tickets through his thick glasses.

"I never win on these damn scratchers. I don't know why I keep foolin' with 'em."

"You never know," the young girl working the counter says.

I've seen this kind of guy around town forever. He hits the occasional twenty- or fifty-dollar winner. Twice a year he hits what he calls "the big time" which is somewhere between a hundred and two-hundred-and-fifty bucks. Around what he spends on tickets a month. He'll go home and take his wife out to dinner and be right back here the next day blowing the rest on some high-dollar tickets that won't payout. He plays the birthdays of his kids and his wife on the daily three times a week, hoping for the big break that will never come. We all find our own ways to kill the loneliness.

"Not today," the old man says. He turns around to see me waiting behind him. "The big winner is all yours, kid."

"Thanks."

"Mmmm" is his only response. Thirty dollars lighter and no hope in sight.

"May I help you, sir?"

She calls me sir, but I'm pretty sure we went to high school together. She's younger than me, but not by much. She has one of those handmade buttons on her apron that holds a picture of two kids smiling at whatever age it is that kids' smiles look like jack-o-lanterns.

"I'd like to cash this receipt in from the coin machine and maybe check on a bus ticket."

I fumble handing her the receipt with the change jar still under my arm. I manage to hand it to her without dropping the jar then I set the jar on the counter. The thought of it crashing to the ground into thousands of pieces whips through my head. I see myself on my hands and knees scraping glass shards into my tee shirt. The glass slipping through my fingers like grains of sand.

When she responds, her voice shakes me back to reality.

"Here you are, sir."

She counts the bills out on the counter. Fanning them out so the dollar amounts are all visible. She sets the penny on the top.

"Eighty-seven dollars and one cent."

"Thank you."

"It's my pleasure. Was there anything else that I could help you with today?"

"Yes, I wanted to check on the price of a bus ticket to the city. One way."

"Sure thing. Let me check my computer here."

She moves and clicks the mouse a few times and is quick with a response.

"$46.50 one way. With a bus change in Merrillsville."

"What days does it come through?"

"Three times a week, Tuesdays, Thursdays, and Sundays. The bus leaves the parking lot at 8pm."

"Thank you."

"Not a problem, sir. Would you like to purchase a ticket today?"

"No thank you. I was just checking."

"Have a good day, sir. And thanks for coming in."

I pick my change jar up off of the counter and head for the automatic doors.

$46.50. That's it. Even with just the little bit of money I had saved it was doable. All I needed was a few more dollars and the guts. You build these things up in your mind so much that even the smallest actions seem impossible. But people do these things every single day. Move to new cities. Buy houses. A second chance and a new beginning. $46.50.

Chapter 51

Josh,

I'm writing this while sitting in the living room, which I haven't been able to see the same way since you visited. I did clean it up a little after you were here. You helped me see things through some clearer eyes. And not just the apartment. I went and checked on bus tickets today and I feel like I can see the light at the end of the tunnel. I have to tell you about my friend Marge when I have more time. She's been inspiring me to get outside of my head. I don't want to sit here dying while there's a world out there to see. Anyway, I just wanted to give you the heads-up that you can expect me sooner rather than later.

The newest Memory Currency *got delivered to work yesterday. I'm only a couple pages in, but I'm really enjoying it. Really dig the new drawing of Captain Jane!!! This is a good chance to test my working theory of her being the physical representation of the author introducing a new idea—not to the readers but to himself. Or maybe I'm just crazy. I'll let you know either way.*

I hope you're well.

Henry

Chapter 52

I am walking into the kitchen when I hear the sound of breaking glass at the front door. By the time I reach it, the door has swung open and Rick, Kaitlyn's dad, is standing there. He has stitches in his face and is breathing heavy. His eyes are wide and wild.

"MOTHER FUCKER!" he shouts.

I am frozen in the suddenness of it all.

"Henry! I've been looking for you!"

"What do you want, Rick?"

My actual voice sounds much calmer out loud than the one inside my head.

"I want you to pay for these fucking stitches in my face to start. And then we're going to settle up."His voice is thick and drunk.

Rick pulls a large hunting knife from the back of his jeans. He starts waving the knife in front of his face like we've all seen in movies. He takes a step towards me and stumbles. I might laugh if I wasn't so scared.

"I was trying to help you out in your shit life and you pull something like this on me?" He gestures towards his face with the knife. "We both could've made a little money."

"Relax, man. What do you want?"

I am strangely unfazed by the threat his presence represents. A perk of my childhood.

"Sit the fuck down ..."

"There's nothing here worth taking, Rick. Look around."

I sit down on the red milk crate in the middle of the living room.

If this were one of my mom's detective shows, I'd be yelling for the person playing my part to grab something and hit him with it or to run away. To do anything but just sit here and find out what happens next. Rick walks in circles around me, still breathing heavy. I can smell the alcohol coming off of him. He walks up slowly behind me, leans over, and puts the knife to my throat. I can taste his breath as he puts his face next to mine. It almost makes me sick.

"Give me your money."

I don't move but I can still feel the wad of bills in my pocket. The thought of handing it over to him makes my stomach turn. Finally I fumble around, pulling it out, and the bills fall to the floor.

Rick takes the knife away from my throat and tells me to pick them up and count it.

"It's eighty-seven dollars."

"Count it."

"I did. Earlier. Twice."

"Hand it to me."

"Fuck you, Rick."

"What did you just say to me? You better watch your mouth, you little shit. Or I'll slit your throat right here in your own house."

"Then do it. Right now. Stop fucking around and kill me then. I have nothing to offer you. I have nothing to offer anyone. That money laying on the floor is everything that I have. And if you want it that bad I'll give it to you. But then you have to leave."

I reach slowly to the floor and gather the bills together. I fold them and hand him them over to Rick while trying to think what Josh would do if he were here. Rick starts counting the money himself, talking out loud. Still holding the knife in his hand.

“Are you done now?” I am disgusted by the whole thing. I just want him to leave. The money means almost nothing to me in that moment.

“Almost. But first I’m gonna cut your face just like you fucked up mine. Then we’ll be even.”

He stuffs the money into his pocket and the thought of how long it had taken me to save it up runs through my head. How many hours at the store I’d spent to get that money. The assholes I’d dealt with and how many times I cleaned the restrooms.

“You have the money. Now just get out of here. Please.”

“And let you walk away from this,” he gestures again towards his face.

His face was worse off than I had thought it would be. There was a steady line of dark, blood-crusted stitches that started at the bridge of his nose and went all the way up into his forehead. He was dirty in general, I could see now, and the stitches looked ragged. The ends splaying out like spider legs over his cracked leathery face.

He bends down over top of me and puts the knife to my face. I feel the point of the knife pressing into my skin and my eyes start to water.

"Go fuck yourself," I spit.

I feel the point of the knife penetrate my skin at the same point his stitches start. The blood comes out onto the surface and I feel a drop roll down my cheek. That droplet of blood finally ignites my fight or flight instinct and I roll off of the milk crate and onto the floor.

"Fuck you!"

"We can get this over with or we can drag it out. I've got nothing else to do today. And give me your fucking wallet."

I can actually see the stream of blood running down my face out of my left eye. They say you can actually always see your own nose but your eyes learn to not pay attention to it. I can see it now.

Rick doesn't jump me while I'm on the floor. He backs off and stands between me and the front door. I stand up slowly keeping my eyes on him and scanning around the room for some kind of weapon. There is nothing.

"Just give me the wallet and I'll leave. I was just fucking around."

The sight of blood has changed his mood immediately. Just like when Ricky pulled the trigger that night at the store.

He has scared himself, finding out how far he could go, how far he had already went.

These mood swings are common with addicts. Love to despair, jubilation to death, glee to an anger to kill in seconds. It's part of what makes them so dangerous. Also, the whole *I was just fucking around* bit. He's already framing the apology, the excuses. If I were to see him later tonight, he probably try and convince me this was all just a misunderstanding. A joke between friends.

I take a moment to weigh my options. I have none. I reach into my back pocket and pull my wallet out. I toss it across the room to him.

I'm surprised when he catches it. I immediately wish I would have thrown it across the room to make him choose between me or the wallet. Why do these ideas always come too late?

He opens my wallet and starts flipping through it.

"Don't worry. I won't take your free coffee punch card."

He pulls my ID out of my wallet and skims over it.

"Henry Sterling, huh? You any relation to Catherine Sterling?"

"She's my mom."

He puts my ID back in the wallet and tosses it back across the room to me. I half-heartedly reach to catch it, while still keeping my eyes on Rick. The wallet bounces off of my hands and falls to the floor. I leave it where it lands.

"Your mom?"

"Yeah. Will you please get out of here? I'm not going to call the cops if that's what you're worried about."

"I was just fucking around, man."

"Just please go."

"I thought you'd have more fight in you."

We stand here in the living room staring at one another. The blood has stopped and I can feel it starting to dry and crust on my face. His stance has steadied and he has a sincere look on his face that I haven't seen from him before.

He laughs quietly to himself.

"I'll see ya around, son."

He turns and heads towards the door, letting the hunting knife fall from his hand to the ground. He leaves the door open on his way out.

Chapter 53

The world has always had a way of disposing of people like me. Somewhere we could work our lives away without giving it much thought. People generally stayed quiet and pacified and eventually retired with enough money to buy a boat or vintage car to work on to pass the time until they died. But now the factories are all gone, but the people are still here. Lost and searching. Now all of the anger that has been bubbling below the surface is starting to reveal itself. And it's ugly. The dinner-table racism that has always existed has gotten louder over the last couple of years. People have been driving around with confederate flags on their pickup trucks here in Brooksville all of my life. We're two hours away from the Canadian border. These flags have nothing to do with anyone's heritage. It's all about the color of people's skin. The people around here vote conservative because they're afraid of change and at the same time, they claim to hate the way things are.

How do you talk someone out of irrational anger and fear?

I think in some ways I owe my grandfather more thanks than I know.

He showed me a lot about how not to be or live.

My generation was told no. Over and over again. We were told what we shouldn't do. But no one had much of an idea of what we should be doing. I grew up in analog. Telephones mounted on kitchen walls with curly cords. The world was changing and the adults were scared. So they told us no while trying to buy themselves some time to figure out what was happening in the world around them. They hit us to keep us quiet while they thought it all over. And when the answers didn't come, they yelled out of frustration and fear.

And so I learned to keep my mouth shut in fear of ever saying the wrong thing.

Chapter 54

I stand in my living room trying to process everything that has just transpired. The crusted blood on my face, the knife laying on the floor by the door, the fact that this man has just called me his son after breaking into my apartment and putting a knife to my throat. I sink to the floor. I try to concentrate on the ceiling fan and the small cord that hangs down from it slowly circling above me from the breeze blowing in through the still-open door.

It's mid-June and I'm 11 years old, playing left field in the most important game of the year. It's the bottom of the sixth inning and there are two outs. The pitcher winds up and the hitter pops a high, lazy fly ball out to left. I move under it and my heart starts to flutter at the thought that I am making the game-winning catch. I can see it landing in my glove before throwing my hands in the air and running towards the infield and the rest of the team running to tackle me in excitement.

I can taste the ice cream in my mouth. I can smell the leather from my glove. The smell of dirt from the field and the faintest whiff of hamburgers grilling from the other side of the park. But as the ball stops its upward motion and begins making its way down to me, I lose it in the late afternoon sun. And it's gone. Terror overtakes the feeling of joy as I scramble in desperation. Suddenly, a crack to the left side of my skull.

The next thing I remember is sitting on the bench in the dugout with ice on my head. The players and parents have all left. Just me on the bench and the coach asking if my mother was on her way. I promise the coach she is on her way. I refuse a ride home and when he is gone I start the three-mile walk home in the dark.

When I finally walk through the door there is no one home and the lights are all out. I take off my uniform and leave it laying on my bedroom floor. I crawl into the shower and let the warm water pour over me while praying for death.

I'm shaken back to reality by the sound of my voice softly singing.

"This little light of mine, I'm gonna let it shine. This little light of mine, I'm gonna let it shine."

The door is still open and it's freezing in the apartment. It takes every bit of energy I have to get up off the ground and walk over to close the door. I pick the hunting knife up from the ground. I walk into the kitchen and place the knife in the sink. I look at the clock on the microwave and it says 9:22 PM. I head into the bathroom and strip off my clothes. I turn the hot water on full blast and climb into the shower slowly, easing my skin into the heat. I can feel the point on my face where the tip of the knife went in. It stings at first, but the pain feels good. I'm still singing as I pick up the soap.

Chapter 55

I sit cross-legged in the rear of the store, back by the beer cooler, surrounded by boxes of candy bars, gum, Tic-Tacs, and potato chips. I open a box of Snickers bars and start refilling the open case on the bottom shelf. It's 3:45 AM and things have settled down for the night. The bar crowd has come and gone and the early birds won't start showing up for another hour or so. I take an odd satisfaction in this part of the job. Making everything new again. Putting the pieces back together. Straightening the plastic bags of beef jerky and refilling the rows of candy. It gives me a sense of control. And after the day I've had, some control feels good.

My brain is on autopilot. I am surviving on muscle memory and play acting and honestly, I feel safer here at the store right now than I would anywhere else. My world has been flipped on its axis and I don't know which way was up. Having that knife to my throat was an out-of-body experience. I was watching life play out in front of me. I'm not sure if Rick was really ready to kill me but you can never really tell when someone is going to flip until they do. I keep running it over in my head thinking of all the different ways it could have played out. I could have ran. I could have fought back. I could have done anything except for just sitting there and letting life happen to me.

I stand up and stretch my legs looking to see if anything else needs to be stocked. The rows look clean and put together. It gives me a small sense of satisfaction. I grab the empty boxes from the ground and head towards the door grabbing a pack of Ultimate 100 cigarettes out of the clearance basket on the counter. I walk the boxes out to the dumpster and unwrap the cellophane from the pack of cigarettes. I take one out and find the book of matches in my pocket. I strike the match and light the long bingo cigarette up and inhale deep. I blow the smoke out in a thick cloud and think about my half-sister dying in my arms.

Chapter 56

"Hey, Mom."

"Henry! I didn't expect to see you again so soon. Have a seat in the back. I'll be right there."

My brain was still chasing its tail at full speed when I walked into the restaurant after work. A walk that would usually take me 30 minutes only took me 12. I had walked out of work the second Mel walked in and I hadn't had a moment to feel bad about it yet.

I sit down at the same booth in the back corner as last time. Ray is here again in his booth and he gives a little wave as I pass by, but I don't wave back. Add that to the list of things I can feel terrible about later.

"What'll it be this morning?"

"Do you have a minute to talk, Mom?"

"It's my morning rush right now, Henry. Can it wait?"

"It can't. Can you please just take a break or something? Get someone to cover your tables?"

"Well, okay. Let me tell Sally and I'll be right back."

I rub my temples with my fingers trying to ease the dull ache in my head that I've had since the adrenaline wore off from the knife incident. I can hear my foot tapping under the table, but it's no longer under my command. My body is doing as it pleases with the caffeine and new rush of nicotine. I can smell the stale cigarette smoke on my hands and my coat and I like it.

"What's so important now, Henry? I have tables and I can't afford to miss out on that money."

"Do you know Rick Baker?"

My mother goes quiet. Her face goes slack and the looking over her shoulder at her tables stops immediately at the mention of his name.

"Who?" She pretends to not have heard me. Or maybe she is wishing she has misheard me.

"Rick Baker, Mom. Do you know him?"

"Why are you asking me that?"

"Why won't you answer the question?"

My voice raises slightly, but I pull back.

"Yes, Henry. I knew Rick a long time ago. Back when we were kids."

"Is he my dad?"

"What?"

"Please stop saying what. I know you hear me. Just tell me. Is he my dad?"

"Henry."

"Henry what? Why can't you answer me? You can't even look at me right now. Is he my father?"

"Why do you care, Henry? It doesn't matter. Look at you, you're doing great."

"I promise you, Mom. I am not doing great."

I had started to raise my voice again and noticed the customers and cooks looking back at us. I take a deep breath and try to calm myself down. I start in again, quieter this time.

"Is Rick Baker my dad?"

My mother takes a deep breath and I just now notice where I got it from. This non-verbal calm-down routine. I make a mental note to never do it again.

When she looks up, I can see she is crying. And seeing your mother cry is one of the few things in this world that I can understand someone killing over. This is actual crying from real hurt. My heart breaks as my consciousness pulls back onto the entire scene. Me and my mother in this booth. Ray next to us staring off into the distance. The customers trying to not look back at us, but also wanting to hear our conversation.

Her shoulders start to heave as her crying grows heavier. I get up and slide in next to her on her side of the booth. I put my arm around her and pull her close to me. For the first time, I can see that she's still the same little girl she has always been. Both of our worlds have shattered to pieces. There's nothing left to hide behind. She is defenseless as a child and it breaks my heart again. I start to cry and tell her everything is ok. That I just needed to know.

She grabs a napkin from the silver dispenser on the table and starts dabbing her eyes. She takes another deep breath and quietly says "I'm sorry."

"It's ok, Mom. I just needed to know. You didn't do anything wrong. And I love you."

"Yes, Henry. He is your father."

She waits a beat and meets my eye through her own tears.

"I'm sorry."

Chapter 57

We sit there together in that back booth and she tells me the whole thing. More than you would ever want to hear from your mother. I knew her father was an awful human, but I hadn't realized how bad it had really been for her. When she explained it to me when I was younger, she would still use cutesy little kid words, even when she was really talking about being raped. Not only by her father, but his brother as well. She told me how her parents would send her off to her cousin's house for weeks at a time, how her uncle would rape her and then laugh about it around the dinner table. How her mother knew it was going on, but was too scared for the both of them to say anything. How the night before she met my father, her father had come into her bedroom in the middle of the night and forced himself inside her.

I stay quiet as she talks, even though my stomach is wrenched. I try to just listen, pulling her close during the hardest parts.

She tells me how Rick had walked into the pizza place she was working at and how handsome he looked in his uniform. A vision of safety and respect. And by the time she served him his third beer and he started flirting with her, she was already in love.

She never went home.

She went back to the hotel with him that night after work. After the first few days, Rick told her he was done with the military, that he wasn't going back. She knew that was bad and tried talking some sense into him, but he wouldn't listen. He had started drinking again the night they met and except for a short stay in a military prison, he hadn't stopped since. He hit her for the first time on their third day together. At first she cried when he did it, but then it kind of made her feel grown up in a sick way.

"I was so young and it happened so long ago. It feels like a different lifetime. I was a child trying to make adult decisions. By the time I knew I was pregnant with you he had already left to try and find a way out of the Army. I honestly thought he had stayed in and would never come back. And then, one day a couple weeks ago, he just comes walking in here. I thought about telling you. I really did. But I had talked to him and he said he was only going to be here for a few days and I figured what was the sense. It would only upset him and disappoint you. I thought he would just go away again."

We sat in the booth for two hours. Taking turns talking and being quiet. The clink of glasses and silverware going on around us. One of the waitresses brought over two slices of cherry pie and two glasses of water. When I stand up to leave my mom stands up with me and straightens her apron. We hug each other tighter than I can ever remember. She looks me in the eye and smiles softly before wiping her tears away and turning and walking back to the kitchen.

Chapter 58

They stayed at that hotel for two weeks. It started soft and sweet, but within a few days it turned sour. They barely knew each other and here they were stuck in a hotel room together, neither one of them having anywhere else to go. Going back home wasn't an option for either of them. My mom kept going to school and work, while Rick stayed in the hotel room drinking. He would usually be blacked out or passed out by the time she got back to the room. The kindness would leave him and he would get angry. Angry at his father for ditching him and angry at my mother for "trapping him."

My mom was just 17 though, and she thought she was in love, so she looked past all that.

On their 13th day together, Rick told her he was running out for cigarettes and would be right back. My mom initially thought he had gone out drinking without her, which upset her but she understood. She spent the night cleaning and organizing the hotel room as best she could to make it feel like a home, while also planning how to sneak into her parent's house to get her clothes and the dress she wanted to wear to the courthouse to marry Rick. She had bought it the year before for a school dance after saving up her money from the pizza place for months but had only had the chance to wear it that one night. She fell asleep on the still-made bed, waiting for him, telling herself not to cry while the late-night talk shows played on the TV.

When she woke up in the morning, Rick was still gone. His G.I. duffel bag was still laying on the floor. And while everything inside of her told her to meltdown she had chosen not to. She had decided to stick to the plan as best she could. What else was she going to do? She threw up before brushing her teeth with the toothbrush Rick had left and shrugged it off to nerves.

After managing to get in and out of her parents' house with no problem, she went back to the hotel and dropped off her things. She had taken what she could carry, nothing more. She sat it down on the floor and went through Rick's duffel bag to see if there was anything worth saving. She found $200 in cash in an envelope and a few green t-shirts with the word ARMY printed on the front that were worth saving. She put the rest back in the bag, slung it over her shoulder, walked outside to the dumpster at the back of the hotel and tossed it in. Then she went to the front desk to see how much longer the room was paid for. It was her first lucky break in a while. Rick had paid for the room for the month, which left her two weeks to figure out her next move. She went back to the room, showered, and went to work.

Over the next two weeks, she quit high school, found an apartment, and realized she was pregnant with me. She was 17 years old.

Hearing all of this put me in awe of my mother. I can't fathom handling that situation at 28, let alone 17. She was a child herself, just trying to survive.

Humans can do amazing things when they're not busy being terrible.

Chapter 59

Henry,

I was finishing a letter to you when I received your latest one in the mail. I was going on about your apartment and the bad vibes it had given me. Like a hotel you were getting ready to check out of. I'm glad my eyes were able to give a new perspective. Did you buy a bus ticket? Or just check on them? Just pull the trigger, man. We can figure everything else out when you get here.

I can't wait to hear more about your friend Marge. It sounds like she's given you some hope. Your last letter was the most positive one you've written to me in years.

This whole Memory Currency thing has really thrown me through a loop. I thought we were reading some sci-fi trash and it turns out we're actually dealing with some high art kind of stuff. I went to the library and checked out a few of the old issues and started picking up on a few other of the author's tricks. It's too much to get into now and I'm still trying to figure it out for myself, but I can't tell you how happy it makes me that sticking with this thing for so long is finally having some kind of intellectual payoff.

Ok. My hand's tired. I'm really happy that you're coming around, Henry. I'll see you soon.

Your friend,
Josh

Chapter 60

I am a product of pain. To not acknowledge that would be irresponsible. This is a large part of what has kept me from ever chasing a romantic relationship with anyone. To think that I have the ability inside of me to create the kind of the pain that my mother experienced terrifies me. And meeting my father only adds to this anxiety. I've felt enough pain in my life to know the last thing I would ever want to do is cause pain to others. It scares me to think of what's inside me, and I think I would want to kill myself if the worst of my roots ever started to come out.

Chapter 61

"Large coffee please. Black."

Hank behind the counter hands me my change and says nothing. He gives me my coffee and I make my way to the back of the shop where I see Marge sitting at a table staring down at a fully set chess board.

"Waiting for someone?"

"Henry! What a pleasant surprise."

"Are you already playing someone or is it ok if I sit?"

"Please, sit, sit. I've always wanted to learn to play but I was always too scared to ask anyone to teach me. I didn't want to seem stupid. So I've decided to teach myself. Do you know how to play?"

"I know how to play, but I'm not very good."

"I'd say that makes us about equal then. I'm the white pieces which, if I've read correctly, means I go first."

"That sounds right."

"My arm hurt for three days after bowling." I tell her while rubbing my shoulder.

"Me too! I'm so glad to hear you say that. I figured it was because of my age."

"I don't think so. It's a completely unnatural motion."

"Is that a cut on your nose?"

"Yeah. It's a long story that ends in me meeting my dad for the first time. Well, not meeting him for the first time but the first time knowing he was my dad."

"Are you ok?"

"I am and I'm not. Kind of everything all at the same time."

"That's a fair sentiment in light of your current situation." Marge says this while eyeing the board for her first move.

"The pawns can only move forward unless they're taking a piece, then they move diagonally. Except on your very first move they can move forward two spaces if you want."

I try explaining without seeming bossy. I hate it when people talk down to me when I'm learning something new.

I knew how all the pieces moved, but it had been a long time since I'd had anyone to play with. I did know one specific strategy that if I remembered correctly, you can usually beat a beginner in the first four or five moves. It was my only go-to, so I went with it.

"May I ask how you stumbled upon meeting your father?"

"He broke into my house. Before he knew I was his son. He was trying to rob me. He cut my nose with his knife because my friend Josh had hit him with a beer bottle."

"That sounds like we're missing a few details."

"We are. And that girl that got hit downtown last week? She was my sister."

I slide a specific pawn out trying to remember the exact moves of the play. Marge makes her second move and I can see the strategy taking shape. We go back and forth with our opening moves and I think I mess up the actual play, but I do seem to have her king pinned from what I can see. I slide my Bishop into place.

"Check."

"Shit," says Marge. She slides her queen out to protect her king and I take it.

"Checkmate, I think."

"Already?"

We both sit staring at the board making sure that it really is a checkmate and after a pretty thorough inspection, we decide that it is.

With an abrupt sweep of her arm, Marge sends all the pieces scattering across the floor. It startles me at first, but when I look up, she's laughing harder than I have ever seen anyone laugh. Everyone in the place, including Hank, is staring at us with disapproval. She stands up and shouts to all of them.

"Oh, relax! We're just playing a game."

I stand up and yell "Checkmate!!!" in Hank's direction.

And we both laugh even harder.

"It sounds like you've lived a lot of life in the last couple weeks. Anything you want to talk about?" Marge asks after we calm down.

"It's all so much right now. I think I'm still processing everything. I don't even know where to begin with it."

"I can understand that. Now get down here and help this old lady pick these little guys up, huh?"

I kneel down and start gathering up the pieces from the floor. Reaching underneath the couch and chairs to wrangle a runaway knight. We're still laughing as we move around on the floor searching for the last of the pieces.

"I always was a sore loser."

"I found a horse. I should've let the game go on longer. I only played that move because it's the only one that I know. I was enjoying the game."

"It does seem that you're always quick to get to the conclusion, Henry. Maybe something to think about."

We put the last of the pieces back onto the board in no real order and sit back down. Both of us still catching our breath.

"That was fun. Thank you for entertaining my new hobby."

We settle back down into our chairs and Marge reaches into her purse, looking for something. When her hand comes out, she places an envelope on the table between us.

"This is for you, Henry. I've been so excited to give it to you. I went out and got it right after our trip to the bowling alley. I know this may seem a little bit forward but it's just going to have to be forward. I've felt a real bond with you over the last few months. And after our last conversation, the idea just hit me and I couldn't stop myself."

She slides the white envelope, which has a picture of a skinny-looking dog on the front of it, across the chessboard.

"Open it."

I open the envelope, peeling the flap away from the glue-sticky seal. I remove the contents, which look official.

"What is it?"

"That's a bus ticket, Henry. Or more precisely, a voucher for a bus ticket. You can go as far away as two-hundred dollars will take you. I've checked around and two-hundred dollars will get you pretty far on a bus."

"I don't know what to say. I .... I just don't know what to say. I don't think I can accept this."

"From what you've been telling me it seems like getting away for a bit is the exact thing you need right now."

"I don't know what to say," I say again. My voice cracks as I speak. My eyes are welling up and as much as I don't want to cry there's nothing I can do. I feel the tears start to run down my face.

"You don't have to say anything, Henry. Just promise me that you'll use it. Soon. If I'm going to sit here with you and tell stories about myself, I'm going to need you to go out and make some stories of your own. A sparring partner is only good when they can keep up with you. Just promise to use it. And to come back sometime and tell me what happens to you. It's as much for me as it is for you. It makes me happy to give it and brightens my day. You get to go out into the world and experience something. We both win."

"I'll never be able to thank you enough for this."

"You don't have to, Henry. Go and live. Get your heart broken.

Make some mistakes. Nothing aspirin and sleep won't fix. And try to enjoy the journey. Look out new windows. See people that are different from you that have no expectation of you. And don't always rush to the conclusion."

"Thank you, Marge."

"You're welcome, Henry."

I hug Marge with an honesty I have previously never known. We say goodbye and I start for the door.

"Oh, Henry. I wanted to ask, what's your last name?"

"Sterling."

"Huh. Thanks. I was just wondering."

As I walk out the door of the coffee shop and stand on the sidewalk. I slip the sunglasses I took from the Lost and Found at work out of my pocket and put them on, even though the sun is now hidden behind the clouds. It feels pretty good. I like the way the darkness of the glasses brings the volume of life down a couple of notches.

Chapter 62

How to get to and then on top of the jewelry store in Brooksville, Ohio:

1. Make a left out of the coffee shop. Take your next left down the side street and then a left down the "alley with no name."

2. Climb up the fire escape. Go slow. The ladder is rusty and will cut into your hands. Be careful of your footing on the rungs. The fourth rung from the top is loose.

3. Pull yourself up and swing a leg over and onto the pebble-covered roof.

4. If possible, try to do this with a bus ticket in the pocket of your jeans and your new sunglasses on. It's the best way to do it.

5. When you get up to the top, be careful not to step on the used needles. Take a moment to admire the sun coming out from behind the clouds.

6. Walk to the ledge and take a deep and honest breath with your eyes closed.

7. Look south down Main Street.

8. Remember there is nothing more to life than being alive.

Chapter 63

It's funny how with each season's change you completely forget that the other seasons exist.

The winters seem to last forever and the sun stays behind the clouds for such extended periods of time that you forget the simple sensation of warmth on your skin.

The feeling of it not being painful to breathe. Standing up here with the town below me, the world feels brand new.

Chapter 64

"It's a pocket knife. It was your grandfather's. I've wanted to give it to you for a long time, I just never found the right moment."

I'm sitting on the couch in the living room of my mother's apartment holding the small box she has just handed me, running my index finger over the smooth worn wood. I open it and see a pocket knife with a deer-in-a-field scene on the handle. It looks like something you could have ordered from Home Shopping Network back in the nineties. I don't tell her this in fear of hurting her feelings. I can tell this is a meaningful gesture to her and I don't want to ruin the moment by being ungrateful.

"Thank you." I say.

"Your grandfather always carried one everywhere he went. He didn't leave me much when he died, but I found a few of these in the attic. That one was in a nice box, so I figured it was a good one. Something to hang onto, ya know? I thought I would give it to you when you got old enough. But then you got old enough and I kind of forgot. But, here it is now. He wasn't all bad, ya know? He could be really kind and thoughtful sometimes. It was a different time."

I run the index finger of my right hand over the small cut Rick left with his knife on my nose.

"I don't think that's true, Mom. I think you and Grandma knew he was angry and dangerous then just as much as you know it now. He wasn't a good person. It doesn't matter what time he lived in."

"Maybe you're right. But that's a hard thing to figure out when you're in the middle of it, ya know? When you're used to things being fucked up, fucked up just becomes your normal. And then where are you? You don't know which way is up anymore. I wanted to be good for you, Henry. I really did. But I just didn't know how. I was too young. Too scared."

"Did you ever dream of anything more? More than Brooksville?"

"My dream would've been to have the time to dream. To have had that time you see in movies where little kids are in their rooms all by themselves just playing. Using their imagination. There was never any time for that in my life. Even as a child. If I was at home I was scared. Scared that my dad was home. Scared that my dad was on his way home. Scared that he had left and was never coming home. Everyone wants a nicer car and a nice house. I would love to have either of those things. But that's not what I'm talking about. I'm talking about being a painter or a fireman or a scientist. I remember when I was little and the kids at school would be talking about their dreams, and even when I was that young I couldn't understand what they meant. I couldn't see that far ahead. When you're 12 years old and worrying about when you're going to eat next and if your dad is going to punch your mom in the mouth tonight or get too drunk and sneak into your bed .... well, the idea of being the president someday never really crosses your mind. It's just not a thought."

She pauses for a breath. "Or maybe I'm just dumb."

"You're definitely not dumb. I think you're brilliant. I think the fact that we're both alive speaks volumes about the person you are. We didn't have it easy, but you always made it work. I know I've been hard on you. But I didn't understand all of these things when I was younger. I knew you were at work and my dad wasn't around. That's all. But I can see the bigger picture now. And I'm sorry it's taken me so long for me to realize it and even longer to say it to you. I didn't appreciate how young you were, that you were just a child yourself. I can't imagine dealing with the things that you have dealt with at any age."

It's invigorating to speak to my mother in this way now. Both of us allowing ourselves to be honest and not hiding behind the old traditional roles of parent and child. We now speak to one another as friends and equals.

"I remember when you were in school and I'd be walking to work and I'd see the kids gathering around for the fights out by that big tree out by the road, near the front entrance to the parking lot of your school. I would laugh because the poor kids had been fighting beneath that tree for as long as I've been alive. Year after year. The poor kids marching out to that tree after school to watch two other poor kids who learned to fight from their parents knock the shit out of each other. It never changes. We become adults and we go to the bars and have a few drinks and before you know it we're heading back outside to fight in the street and the only thing that has changed is the location. And we make these children and we just keep teaching them the same things. And we don't even know that we're doing it. All I wanted was for you to not be one of them. To give you some time to dream. Of something. Anything."

She picks up a pack of cigarettes from the cluttered table and shakes the box. She pulls a cigarette from the pack and places it between her lips. She flicks a small white Bic lighter in her right hand. Her nails are painted a bright red that screams cheap and the polish is cracked and flaking. I want to hug her and tell her how well she has done. For herself and for me. That as hard as it's been, I know it could have been much worse. I want to say all of this to her. But before I can start she exhales a cloud of smoke into the stagnant apartment air and continues.

"I wish I would have known even a quarter of this before I had you, Henry. And I don't mean that in a bad way. You know I love you. But I've watched you grow up. And struggle. And it just seems to me I could have saved you a lot of pain if I'd not had you. And please know how I mean that, Henry. Not hurtful. I just mean, maybe both of us would have had a better chance. I could have kept my bullshit all to myself."

She pauses and flicks the ashes of her cigarette into an ashtray.

"My biggest fear was that you'd end up turning out anything like your grandfather. Every time I see you, it's still like I'm waiting for the light to turn on inside your head and all of a sudden that side of you is just going to kick in. But here you are. I know it doesn't mean much coming from me, but you're a good person, Henry. A really good person with a true heart. And I don't think you have many people to thank for that but yourself."

She takes a last drag off of her cigarette and snubs it out in the ashtray. She picks up a plastic bottle of air freshener from the table and spritzes the air around her.

I take advantage of her pause to jump in.

"I know how hard you had it growing up. And you haven't had it much easier as an adult. You've given me a better shot than what you had. Even if I haven't done the best with the opportunity. Isn't that what being a parent is all about? To make sure your kids have it at least a little bit better than you did? And you did it. You succeeded. And no one made it easy on you either."

"Have you heard or seen from Rick at all?" she asks.

"I think I've heard enough from Rick. More than I cared to, in fact." I touch the cut on my nose again, wondering if I should tell her everything. I decide sometimes the truth doesn't help anyone involved. “I haven’t been exactly looking for him either. Besides, I don’t think he has much to say to me.”

“I’m sorry about that, too.”

“He wouldn’t have done either one of us any good. I’m glad I met him, but I’m also happy to have not had him around for the last 28 years. For both our sakes.”

“Do you have to work tonight?”

“I do. But I came over here to tell you something.”

“Is everything ok?”

“I wanted to tell you that I’m leaving.”

“Leaving? Where?”

“I’m going to the city. I’m heading to the grocery store to buy my ticket right now. I have to check the bus schedule, but I’m thinking I’ll go sometime in the next two weeks. And I think I’m going to quit my job either way.”

“Henry, is that really a good idea? Quitting your job? You can go out of town for a bit without quitting. I’m sure they’ll give you a few days off.”

"I don't think I'm going for a few days. I think it's going to be longer than that."

"What do you mean?"

"I mean I'm leaving Brooksville. And I'm not sure that I'm coming back. There's nothing here, Mom. I can work at a gas station anywhere. I have to go and try and find something for myself. Outside of Brooksville."

"Do you know how expensive it is to live in a city?"

"I don't. But I'll figure it out. And I have to go soon. I was given an opportunity and I'll hate myself if I don't at least try."

"Where are you going to live?"

"Josh said I could stay with him as long as I want. And I'll figure it out from there."

"With Josh?"

Her face is a question mark.

"I'm leaving, Mom. And the last thing I want to do is fight with you about it. You have to understand that I want something more than this. Especially after everything we've just talked about. I don't want to die in this town."

"You're telling me you're going off to someplace you have never been. That you've only ever seen on TV, and you think you're just going to show up and find a place to live and a place to work. You're being ridiculous. And on top of that you're telling me you're going off to live with your friend *Josh*?"

"Yes."

She takes a deep, exasperated breath. She closes her eyes and tries to calm herself. This is why I was afraid to tell her. I don't want to leave with things like this between us.

"Henry, we need to talk about Josh."

Chapter 65

Dear Josh,

Where do I even begin. Rick, Kaitlyn's dad, showed up at my apartment waving a knife around and demanding money after the whole beer bottle incident at the Angry Steer. He took the money I had saved up and put a small cut on the bridge of my nose. Then he found my ID in my wallet. He saw my last name and fuck, it turns out that guy is my fucking dad. He and my mom were together for two weeks before he split town. He left before he even knew my mom was pregnant. My mom told me all that stuff. It was hard to hear, but it made us closer, which is a good thing.

Anyway, my head is a total mess, but the real reason I'm writing is to tell you that Marge bought me a bus ticket. Well, a $200 voucher for a bus ticket. I couldn't believe it when she gave it to me. I still don't know how I'm going to thank her, but I'm so excited I had to sit down and write you as soon as I got home.

I'm sorry. I'm a little unfocused right now, as you can probably understand. When I told my mom I was leaving, she didn't take the news very well. She threw a fit and I walked out. I'm hoping she'll come around to the idea though. I'll just have to wait and see.

One last thing. On page 14 of the newest Memory Currency, Captain Jane is drawn with blue hair. On the next page, she's living underwater with that one weird character that's human but has crab claws instead of hands. I can't think of his name at the moment. Anyway, my theory seems to be holding up under scrutiny so far.

I know this is a lot all at once. We can sort it out face-to-face soon. I'll let you know more after I buy my ticket.

Henry

Chapter 66

The Map:

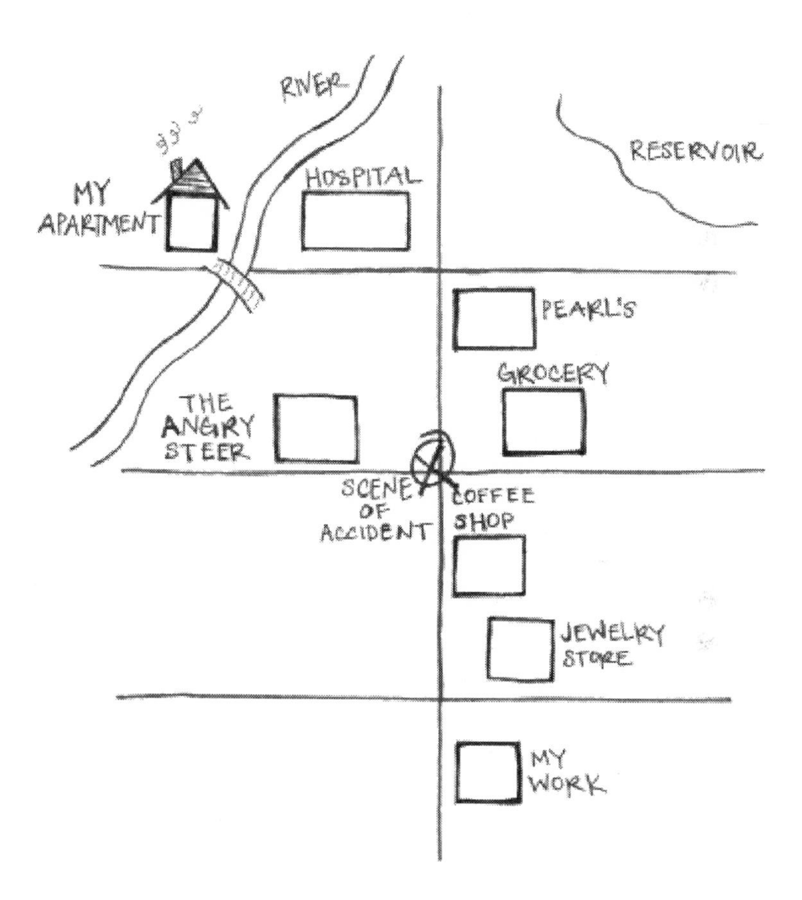

This is a map of Brooksville. The 3.2 square miles that I have spent my entire life within.

I grew up bouncing around from apartment to apartment on the far northeast side. I've tried to mark all of the places that I frequent. The coffee shop, the store where I work, the crosswalk where Kaitlyn died. The Angry Steer is to the west off Main Street, the place where Nicky Halcourt killed Kevin Hines and where Josh hit Rick with the beer bottle. The jewelry store, the restaurant my mom works at, it's all here.

I always feel more connected to something when I can see it in front of me, so I thought a map might help you too.

This is all I know of the world. I only know one person who lives outside of this drawing.

Chapter 67

There's still a chill in the air from the wind that blows down from the north, but the March sun is warm. I zip up my thin windbreaker and make a left outside my mom's door, moving down the sidewalk. My mom is still sitting at the table, asking me not to leave as I close the door.

In my left pocket my hand is wrapped around my grandfather's pocket knife. In my right pocket is the bus ticket voucher.

A half-block away from my apartment, I come to the small bridge that crosses the river. I stand on the bridge facing north, looking down, watching the water run underneath me.

I pull the knife from my pocket and hold it in my hand. It feels cheap. It's the kind of thing that looks nice and shiny from far away. Through a glass case, maybe. But then it falls apart in your hand the first time you try to use it. I slide my fingernail into the small divot in the blade and pull it out. You could never use this knife to cut anything. It's so flimsy that you couldn't even butter bread with it and the silver paint on the blade would come off the second you tried to wash it. I close the blade and feel the weight of the knife in my hand. I carry enough memories inside of me. I have no need for physical reminders of my disposability.
I reach back and toss it as hard and as far as I can. It arcs up and out over the water and lands with a small thud in the spring mud on the bank of the east side of the river. Some kid will find it now and be happy to have it.

I continue on my way back to my apartment. But when I get there, my feet keep moving east. My mind is a carnival ride and the person in the seat is about to be sick. I cross over Main Street to the east side of town. The smell of mud fills the air as the ground has begun to thaw with winter winding down. I can feel myself sweating inside of my thin jacket and am happy for the feeling. I cut through the grocery-store parking lot towards the entrance. The conversation with my mom is still zigging and zagging through my brain. I'm sad that it turned ugly on us both. I decide that saying all that was maybe her way of saying goodbye without having to actually say it. After talking with her, I knew it was finally time to go. We had gotten as close as we were ever going to be and it wasn't a closeness that was going to save either of us.

Inside, I'm enveloped by the bright lights of the store, the primary colors of the packaging, the low-level hum of air-conditioning units, the chattering of voices. The sucking sound of the automatic doors closing behind me acts like a seal.

I make my way over to the service counter and smile when I see that the same old man is here again buying lottery tickets. Bent over the counter scratching the little bit of money he has away, hoping for a miracle. Maybe the act of scratching the ticket is his miracle. His respite from the world.

The world told him to work hard and the preacher told him to sacrifice and he did all that and now here he stands crumpled over the counter with a bad back, a small pension, and a million complaints about how all he ever did was work hard and sacrifice.

I move into line behind him and watch him scratch and brush whatever that silver stuff is that you scratch off the tickets onto the floor. He has a green scratcher in his right hand. It's a tiny plastic paint scraper that the big players use for scratching their tickets. The sign of a real pro.

"Shit. Nothin' again."

He breathes a deep sigh and tries to smile at the girl behind the counter.

"Maybe tomorrow," she says returning the smile.

The old man shuffles off into the grocery part of the store, probably going to pick up the milk that was his excuse for being here in the first place. He'll buy a half gallon instead of the gallon and come back and spend the two bucks he's saved on a couple of the daily Pick 4s.

They both seem happy for the routine. Him and the girl behind the counter. It's something they can depend on. I know how that feels. Even when we complain about our routines, we're secretly happy to have them. Besides, without those routines, what's left?

I'm watching the scene play out and trying to decide whether the whole interaction is terribly depressing and sad, or absolutely beautiful when the girl behind the counter interrupts my train of thought.

"May I help you, sir?"

Chapter 68

"How are you today?" I ask. Trying to buy myself time.

"I'm doing well. Is there anything that I can help you with today?"

I pull the ticket voucher from my right pocket. It's damp from being clenched inside of my hand on the walk over here, and the refrigeration of the grocery store makes the wetness even more pronounced.

I hand the voucher to her almost unconsciously, hoping the deal is still real.

"And what kind of ticket are you looking for today? Where are you heading?"

"The city," I say. Trying to sound like I have done anything like this before in my life.

"I think this more than enough to cover the ticket."She says it with a reassuring smile.

"Okay. Let me see here. And when you were looking to leave?"

"I was thinking next week, maybe?"

"Let's see, I have a bus next Thursday at 8PM. It looks pretty open right now. How does that sound?"

"Perfect."

"8 PM on Thursday. And would you like to book your return ticket now also?"

"I might hold off on that for now, if that's ok?"

"Of course. That's no problem. Just let me get your ticket printed out and you'll be all ready to go .... so what's taking you to the city?"

"Nothing really. I just kind of wanted to check it out. See someplace new. Have you ever been?"

"When I was little my parents would take me and my brother to go shopping or to see movies. I haven't been in a long time. Too many people for me. Too many strangers. But maybe you'll like it."

"Can I ask you a question?" I surprise myself with this interruption.

"Sure. What can I help you with?"

"Well, it's actually kind of a personal question. Not real personal or anything. Kind of generally personal."

"Okay."

"Do you like your job here?"

"I mean, I guess so. I've been working here for five years and I haven't quit. The people are nice enough. And it keeps my bills paid. What else is there really?"

"I don't know."

"Neither do I."

We're silent for a moment, but for some reason, it's not awkward at all.

"Ok, gimme just a minute then. I have to run back into the office to get your ticket out of the printer."

She walks back to the office behind a plexiglass wall and I can see her standing at the machine, waiting for the ticket to print out.

She stands with one hand on her hip like she's bored by the process, like she's done it a million times before. She reaches behind her back to adjust her bra strap before remembering that I can still see her. She looks back out at me and smiles then pulls the ticket from the printer and walks back out to the counter.

"Here you are. And I wrote your remaining balance on the voucher."

"Thank you so much for your help."

"I hope you have a great trip. And if you figure out when you want to return just come back and see me and we'll take care of it."

"I will. And thank you again. I hope you have a great day."

I walk out of the grocery store with my ticket in hand. Dizzy with excitement and disbelief. Out the front doors and heading back west towards home with my head and body both buzzing. I walk home at almost a running pace. I need to write Josh immediately.

Josh,

I bought my ticket!!! Can you believe it? I leave next Thursday night. I'll get in around 11. Can you pick me up from the bus station?

I have so much I need to do. Tell my landlady and Mr. Clark at work. I won't have much of anything when I get there so I may need to borrow a few things if that's ok. I'm just bringing what I can fit in a backpack. I hope that's ok.

There probably isn't time for you to respond to this by letter so I'll try to call you from work. I just couldn't wait to tell you.

See you soon!

Henry

Chapter 69

When I finish the letter I go to the kitchen drawer and find a stamp and an envelope. I seal the letter up, address it, and immediately walk to the post office.

Chapter 70

That night I walk to work with a renewed sense of purpose. Now that there's an ending to this part of my life it makes me want to feel some nostalgia. The excitement is still bubbling inside of me as I walk through the parking lot at work.

When I get past the gas pumps, I see a beat-up maroon Chevy Corsica sitting in front of the air pump with its engine running and the headlights off. The inside dome light keeps flickering on and off. I walk over to the car just as the dome light flicks back on and I see Gina in the passenger seat crushing up pills on a Chris Gaines CD case.

Her eyes are all over the place as she smiles an unhinged smile and waves furiously at me.

I half-heartedly wave back. I try and smile, but my heart's not in it. I put my head down and walk into work.

Chapter 71

I'm surprised to see that Mel is here again on another double. She's finishing ringing up a lady who's speaking to her in Spanish. I come in at the end of the transaction to hear Mel say in a louder than normal voice, "Have a good night, now!"

The lady smiles as she passes me walking out the door, but doesn't acknowledge Mel.

"You know saying it louder doesn't help her understand you, right?" I ask Mel.

"I know, but I don't know what else to do. She probably thinks I was mad at her. I wish I could speak another language. Too late to try and mess with it now. Could you imagine living in a place where you couldn't speak the language? You can't even tell people to go fuck themselves. I don't know how anyone does it."

"Maybe she was telling you to go fuck yourself?"

"Good for her."

I laugh.

"Alright, I'm gonna finish counting out my drawer and get home. It's been a long day," she says.

"What are you doing here again tonight?"

"That new guy we hired came up eighty bucks short on his first shift. I looked for the money, but couldn't find it and he didn't even mention it to anyone at the end of his shift. I called him five times yesterday and he didn't answer. I'm guessing he had no intention of coming back."

"Damn. I could've come in."

"How were we supposed to get a hold of you? You don't have a phone."

"That's true."

"I need the money anyway. I'm tired as hell though. And I'm taking a six-pack home with me tonight. Can you make it go away on your waste sheet?"

"Yeah. No problem."

I was suddenly nervous with Mel. More than I usually am. I was so excited to tell someone I was leaving but I didn't have anyone else to tell.

"Hey, I wanted to tell you something."

"What's up?"

"I'm leaving. Next Thursday. I'll make some calls and get my shifts covered for the next week so you should be fine here. And I'll let Mr. Clark know, too. I just wanted to tell you myself."

"Where are you going?"

"A friend of mine bought me a bus ticket. I'm gonna try the city for a little bit. I just wanted to tell you so you didn't find out from someone else or have to worry about covering my shifts."

"Is this about the shit at the bar the other day?"

"What? No. You heard about that?"

"Of course I heard about it. Steve came in a couple days ago talking about it. He said it was the dad of that little girl that got hit downtown. Steve said the guy's an asshole. I figured he had to be if he made you do something like that."

"It wasn't me, actually. But, yeah, the guy's a terrible person."

"You don't have to be modest with me. Steve told me what happened. So you're leaving, huh? For good?"

"I think so."

"Good for you, Henry. Come back sometime and tell me about it."

"I will. Have a good night, Mel."

"You too, Henry. Don't smash any customers in the face with any beer bottles. Or do. Fuck 'em."

Chapter 72

The next couple days pass like a cough syrup dream. Fast and slow all at the same time. Life with a halo of nostalgia hanging over my head. The smallest actions become romantic. Sweeping the apartment floor. Filling the candy racks at work. Every conversation with Mel. It's all taken on a new context now that there's an end in sight. It's funny how a change of perspective can put your whole existence in a brand new light.

Chapter 73

A phone call to Josh:

"Are you all packed?"

"Not yet. There's not a lot to pack. I'm just going to set my mattress out on the curb before I go. I told my landlady I was leaving. I have a letter written up to leave here for Mr. Clark. I'm sure he'll understand. I'm hoping he comes in the morning so I can tell him face to face. "

"How are you feeling?"

"Scared, but excited."

“Have you talked to your mom anymore since the last time?”

“I haven’t. She took it harder than I thought she was going to. You wouldn’t believe the things she was trying to tell me to get me to stay. I feel kind of bad but I don’t think we have anything else positive to say to one another.”

“What did she say?”

“We can talk about it when I get there. It’s too much to explain over the phone. You’re going to be there at the bus station to pick me up, right?”

“Of course, I took the day off. Just get on the bus. That’s all you have to do. ”

“I know. I’ll see you at 11 PM at the bus station?”

“I’ll be there.”

I hang up the payphone, walk back inside, and pick up yesterday’s newspaper. I’m halfway through the *Lights and Sirens* page when the front door bell dings. I physically shake when I see that it’s Rick. I set the paper down and stand up. I feel under the counter and touch the handle of the aluminum baseball bat we keep below the register. I watch him walk back to the beer cooler, grab a 30-pack of ‘Stones, and bring them up to the checkout.

He sets the beer on the counter with an audible grunt. When he looks up, I can tell he's surprised to see me. He rolls back on his heels and takes a step back.

We stare at each other, each waiting for the other to speak. I stay quiet, forcing him to speak first.

"Your face alright?" he asks.

"Yeah. Yours?" I say as short as possible.

"Itches more than anything."

We stand in silence for another five seconds. I can tell he is as unready and uneasy to see me as I am him. I have a million things I want to say. Things that I've gone over and over in my mind, but now that he's here, I can't think of a single one.

He sighs and I can hear his nose whistle because of the stitches.

"I know you have every right to hate me." He says defensively. "If it counts for anything your mom never told me about you. I didn't find out about you until they had let me out of the Army. By then it seemed like it was too late. And since she never told me about you, I figured she didn't want me around anyway. I would've just fucked you up more than you already are."

"Thanks." I say smugly. Not that he's wrong.

"You know what I'm saying. Look at me. I'm not meant to be anyone's dad."

"You aren't. Not anymore."

With those words, my anger starts to dissipate. He deserves it, but it's still a cheap shot.

Deep down, I feel sorry for both him and my mom. They were both just lost little kids. Neither had any real guidance or support from their families. They were victims of their upbringing. Just as much as the rest of us.

"Kaitlyn," he says. "She was your half-sister. You didn't know but..."

"I do now," I say, jumping in when he pauses. "I'm glad I didn't know then. It makes the whole thing a little easier."

"But you still cared," he says. "You went to the hospital when you didn't have to, when you didn't even know anything."

His voice trails off and the silence hangs there between us. It's all true and there doesn't seem to be anything else to say.

After a few awkward beats, Rick reaches in his back pocket and pulls out his wallet.

"How much I owe ya?"

I ring up the beer.

"$21.36 altogether."

"Shit. All I have is a $20. Could you spot your old dad a couple bucks?" He says this with a laugh, undercutting any good he did just now by acting like he cared.

"Twenty's fine. Just get out of here." I say.

"Can I ask you a question?" he says, putting his hand on the handle of the case of beer, but still letting it sit on the counter. He won't pick it up until he's good and ready to go. "Why'd you hit me the other night? I know I was a little drunk, but I don't remember saying anything that would've pissed you off that much."

"It was my friend Josh that hit you. He was sticking up for me. That's what people who care about others do. He's a good friend like that."

"Who?"

"Josh. He was there with me. He's the reason I was there in the first place."

"I'm not calling any cops, man. You can put your alibi away. I was just wondering what made you snap? Tequila has always hit me that way too. I guess the apple doesn't fall far from the tree."

He picks the beer up and starts sauntering toward the door, a little bit giddy maybe, about getting off so easy.

"Just get out of here," I repeat, my voice betraying how weary I am with all this, how depressing it is to me to think that I came from him.

"Stay clear of the tequila, kid. Have a nice life."

As Rick shuffles toward the exit, I notice the heel of his right shoe has come unglued. It claps back and forth between his foot and the tile as he walks out. The doorbell dings and the hydraulic door closes slowly behind him.

For a moment, I hate myself for not saying every terrible thing to him that is pulsing through my mind. The thought of that bus ticket waiting for me at home calms me down. I sit down and go back to reading the paper to see how many of the names I know in the *Lights and Sirens* section.

A quarter of the way down the page, I see Ricky Stump's name. It says he was booked into the county jail last night for domestic assault.

I think of Gina and wonder where she is right now. I glance out the window and the street is quiet. All of these broken characters. The movie stars on the covers of the magazines stare back at me from the magazine rack. I think of all the people leading big lives in big cities. Making important decisions. Out here, most of us are crawling over one another for the next fix. The next fuck. The next drink. The next fight. Anything to help us forget what we have done to ourselves, how little we are able to control who we are and what we become.

When I'm shaken from my daydream by the next ding of the doorbell, I'm flicking a red Bic lighter and staring into the flame. My fingernail has turned black and it is 4:14 AM.

Chapter 74

Leaving Day:

"Good morning Brooksville! It's a beautiful Thursday and we're happy you're tuned into WQRC: THE HITS YOU MISS!!! We're going to see a high today of 68 degrees, but it's gonna drop down to a brisk 38 tonight, so don't put those winter coats in the back of the closet just yet.

We've got a long list of birthdays today that we'll get to in just a bit, but first the construction on North Main Street has ended so things will be a little quicker getting through town up by Hospital Hill. Saturday morning there will be a pancake breakfast hosted by the Shriner's Club. 7 until 10:30 benefitting the Brooksville Little League. Also, the Brooksville Patriots girls softball team will host the Melmore Hawks tonight at 6:30 on the south diamond at Brooksville High School.

And don't forget to join us downtown Friday afternoon at 6:30 for the Spring Parade hosted by your very own WQRC. We'll have all of the county's marching bands and all of the Brooksville spring sports teams out to celebrate the end of the long winter. It's fun for the whole family so don't forget to bring the kids.

We'll get to those birthdays in just a few minutes but first, let's hear some hits from the 50s and 60s to get your day started on the right foot. From the days of milkshakes and soda jerks, here's the 1958 classic from the Chordettes, their hit song 'Lollipop.'"

Most days I wake up and reach for the alarm clock. But today the news seems quaint. Knowing that tomorrow everything will be different. I'll be waking up in a new place with a new world in front of me. So today, I try to enjoy it. To find that charm that politicians always talk about being so inspired by in places like Brooksville. The parades that the city council throws what seems like every other day so the people in town have something to look forward to. The mayor, who also owns the only shoe shop in town, thinking that if everyone gathers around Main Street once a month it will somehow return the town to the idealized glory days that he wants to believe really happened. Children waving small American flags while candy gets tossed from the bed of a pickup truck. Happy Friday! At the same time, the local EMTs are using fifteen cans of Narcan a day to revive heroin overdoses.

That would be bad enough, but the town's people are actually trying to pass a regulation to stop the use of Narcan, as if it's somehow encouraging people to overdose.

This is the new Americana.

After the parades, the street sweepers will push all the used needles and broken beer bottles into the gutter to be washed down the storm drain and out into the river. But for a little while before then, the good folk of Brockville will drag their kids out to the curb to watch the parade go by, to celebrate an image and idea of America that has been dead longer than I've been alive.

I sit up in bed and let the song play. "*Lollipop*" by the Chordettes. The Chordettes are amazing singers. The song "Lollipop" is an absolute atrocity. But songs like that help reinforce people's ideas of the world they think they're still living in. Back when they could simply ignore the problems that existed in the outside world. That's why they stay popular. But those days are gone and there aren't enough covered wagon placemats or "Let Go And Let God" wall hangings in the world to stop it. The information is here and it's only getting faster. And it's only getting harder and harder for the people, even in places like Brooksville, to remind themselves of a time when they used to dream.

The last finger in the cheek *pop* of "Lollipop" plays and the song ends.

My day has started on the right foot, apparently.

Up next is a recorded message from the mayor reminding us that he's up for election again in November and that his rival has "no political experience" and even owns a bar in Brooksville. A bar with a "sordid history not suitable for radio." The mayor's monotone drones on about all of the good he has done for the town. He fails to mention that 86% of the children in public schools are living below the poverty line. That there are no private schools left in Brooksville.

"That has to be Steve," I say to myself.

The mayor of Brooksville has contracts with all of the Brooksville school sports teams. He's the owner of the only place within a thirty-mile radius where you can purchase track, football, or baseball cleats. Or a pair of reasonable basketball shoes. He shows up personally to measure the kids' feet in the auditorium, with three different styles to choose from. He shakes the hands of the teachers, coaches, parents, and kids while he's there. Face time, I think politicians call it. The mayor gets plenty of it. This would seem like a conflict of interest to most. I would agree. But no one with any kind of power around town thinks to mention it.

This is how the mayor has kept his position in Brooksville for the last 12 years. Selling outdated and discontinued sports shoes that he buys in bulk for cheap with an immediate resale avenue to the people whose best interests he's supposed to be serving. And he makes the mayoral salary on top of his shoe scheme, doing alright for himself in a place where people don't ask many questions.

The station goes silent for a second after the mayor's message, which ends with an emphatic "And God Bless America!" that feels over the top for a local mayoral race that is followed by the revving motorcycle sounds that kick off "Leader Of The Pack" by the Shangri-Las. I reach over and rip the cord of the clock radio out of the wall one last time for old times' sake.

I shower and get dressed and sit for a few minutes in the living room thinking of where to start with packing up the apartment. I decide throwing everything away is my best course of action. I do a couple passes through the rooms, picking up garbage and any junk I can carry one-handed. It happens quicker than I expect. By the end of my second time through, the place is feeling empty and abandoned. I go to the kitchen and pull everything out of the cupboards and drawers and lay it out on the kitchen counter. There's not much here. A couple plates and a few pieces of silverware. Three plastic bowls. No pots or pans. In the drawers there are some old batteries and paycheck stubs. I throw it all away. The only thing I save is the stack of letters from Josh and the two latest copies of *Memory Currency*.

Next, I move to my bedroom. I go to my closet and lay everything out on the mattress on the floor. I pack two pairs of pants, six t-shirts, five pairs of socks, and five pairs of underwear into a black backpack I've had since high school. Everything else I load into garbage bags and haul out to the communal garbage bin outside on the side of the apartment complex.

The bathroom is already empty except for two towels on the rack, a toothbrush, mouthwash, and a four-pack of razors. I throw the towels away and pack the rest into the front pocket of my backpack.

I am left with only my mattress to dispose of.

I struggle getting it out the door by myself. I go back and forth between awkwardly picking it up and dragging it right side up. It's a struggle but I eventually get it outside and out to the curb.

I go through the apartment with an all-purpose cleaner and a roll of paper towels. I wipe down the sinks in the kitchen and bathroom. The kitchen counter. The fridge is already empty. I wipe down the shelves and drawers inside.

I throw the cleaner away and leave what's left of the paper towels on the kitchen counter. I open a window in the living room and one in the bedroom to let some fresh air in. The air moves through the apartment and makes it feel almost brand-new. The sun is lighting up the rooms as I walk through the place one last time, searching for a feeling of some kind. Memories, good or bad. Some kind of nostalgia. There is none to be found. It's 4 PM.

I don't have to be at the bus stop until 7:30, but I have no more reason to be here. This apartment is no longer mine. It contains no trace of my life or existence, inside or out. It's just some empty rooms now, waiting for another occupant.

I lock the door, put the keys in the mailbox, and pause one last time, hoping for a wave of some kind of emotion to roll over me.

I sit down on the front steps and cram the stack of letters and the copies of *Memory Currency* into my now-stuffed backpack. The zipper doesn't want to go, but I force it as best I can.

I feel aimless. Three hours to kill and nowhere to be. I decide to head east towards downtown.

I make my way to Main Street and turn south. My brain told me the search for any kind of goodbye was over, but my feet apparently feel differently. I walk the couple blocks to the main intersection of downtown and make a right to the west. I'm now standing at the crosswalk where my sister Kaitlyn died while I held her in my arms. I never knew her. The only time I got to spend with her was while she laid here in the street with a badly broken leg and the back of her head bleeding. My guts churn and my chest tightens.

I take a deep breath and blow it slowly out of my mouth. I remind myself of the pain I was saved by not knowing her. I dealt only with her tragic end. None of the messy stuff before that. I hope her life held some happiness, more than mine somehow. That would be good. I want to hope that everything she experienced up until those last moments was good, was what she deserved, but I think that's too much to ask, given what else I know about where she came from, the history we share even though we never really met or knew each other.

The scene replays in my head. The screeching tires. Her little body lying underneath the car. The terrified driver's face. His pleading voice. There I am holding her here in the street. The little silver snow boot laying a few feet away. Her thin coat. Our sad little expendable lives.

The saying used to be *the rich get richer, the poor get poorer*. My mother used to say this all the time to me when talking about work and paying bills.

But that's not the case anymore. It's now *the rich get richer, the poor die*. Poor people anger the rich. Rich people see all poor people as lazy. But growing up poor, I can tell you nothing is further from the truth. Poor people take pride in hard work. It's all that they have to take pride in.

The rich never stop and think that maybe the poor person has to work really, really hard just to have one nice thing for themselves.

A smartphone. A quality pair of shoes. A decent outfit. The rich seem to think that if poor people were just smarter and spent their money more wisely that they would magically pull themselves out of poverty. But that's not how poverty works. Poverty isn't a basement you can choose to leave by walking up the stairs and out whenever you choose. Poverty is a hamster wheel. No matter how long, hard, or fast you run you always end up exactly where you started. Exhausted, broke, and all the worse for the wear. People get dealt bad hands. And they pay for it with their lives.

The rich don't understand this because they, for the most part, have never been poor. My sister Kaitlyn dying in the middle of the street is viewed in most of America as one less mouth to feed.

I think about all of this and her little silver snow boots.

"My sister Kaitlyn." I say out loud. Trying to make it feel real for myself. I adjust the straps on my backpack and look both ways before crossing the street.

On the other side of the street is the bank that my paycheck gets deposited into automatically every two weeks. It's already closed for the day so I go to the ATM on the back side of the building. I put my card in and punch in my PIN.

The screen reads: Available balance: $63.57.

The machine only dispenses 20 dollar bills. I touch the screen a few times and request the 60 bucks. I resolve myself to abandoning the remaining three dollars and fifty-seven cents to the powers that be. The machine spits out the three twenty-dollar bills. I pull them from the machine and place them in my wallet along with my card. This is all of the money I have in the world. I convince myself that's ok and head back towards Main Street.

When I get to the south end of town, I see there's an ambulance and a cop car parked at the gas station store. By now it's almost six o'clock and a pink March sun is barely holding on in the western sky. It's just dark enough that the lights on the ambulance and cop car are visible bouncing off of the surrounding buildings. As I get closer I can see Mel standing outside talking to one of the cops. She's smoking a cigarette and amazingly seems to be not yelling. This seems like a good sign.

The ambulance throws on its sirens as I'm crossing the street. I move a little quicker to the sidewalk on the same side as the store. The ambulance pulls out from the parking lot, hard and quick with a faint screech of tires, accelerating up Main Street towards the hospital.

Mel sees me as I'm walking up and comes toward me.

"What happened?" I ask.

“Some girl OD’d in the bathroom. I had to call the cops.”

“Was she ok?”

“I think so. They busted down the door and I saw them stab her with one of those OD shots. She came to right after that.”

“Do you know who it was?”

“I think it was that same girl that punched you in the head. She a friend of yours?”

“Just an acquaintance.”

“They said she’ll be fine. Right as rain after one of those shots. I wish I had me one. I could’ve used one this morning.”

“I’m not sure that’s how it works.”

“Whatever. So, you’re out of here, huh? When do you leave?”

“Tonight. My bus leaves at 8. I cleaned my apartment out and didn’t know what else to do with myself. I’m just out killing some time before I head over to the grocery store.”

“That’s really great, Henry. I’m glad you’re leaving. Not glad but, you know what I mean.”

"I do," I assure her.

"I should get back in there," Mel says, waving her cigarette in the direction of the store."Good luck, Henry. Don't forget to come back and see us."

"Thanks, Mel."

She throws her cigarette on the ground and stamps it out with the toe of her shoe. Squishing it into the asphalt before turning and heading towards the store. She takes a couple steps and then stops and turns back around. She walks back towards me and moves up close to me. She puts her arms around me and hugs me. Tightly.

"I care about you, Henry. I want you to do well. So get out of here, huh? For all of us."

"Thank you, Mel. That means a lot to me."

We let go of the hug and she takes me by my elbows and looks me in the eye. The purple makeup around her eyes is smeared and I can see she's crying. Neither of us knowing what else to say, so we both nod. She turns and heads back into the store. I stand there in the parking lot, not sure what to do.

My plan was to buy a Coke and a copy of the *Lamplight* for the bus ride, but now I didn't want to ruin the moment after our goodbye.

I decide I can get both at the grocery store.

I start to head back north, towards the grocery store. The sun is fading and it's now much cooler than it was when I left the apartment. I zip my jacket all the way up to my neck. Suddenly, all of this feels real. I'm leaving. Right now. In a matter of hours. The thought occurs to me that I have truly have no idea what tomorrow will bring. My pace quickens and I start to daydream about a new life for myself. Maybe a pair of new shoes, at least.

A white Ford Festiva pulls up in front of me at a cross street. There's a woman driving and she's smoking a cigarette with the windows rolled up. There are two kids in the backseat. Neither in car seats. It shakes me from my daydream. I know things like this happen everywhere in the world. But why in places like Brooksville do they feel like a source of pride?

I wave at the kids in the back seat. They both look tired and don't wave back. I motion for the lady driving to go ahead. She takes a drag from her cigarette and glances both ways before darting across Main Street. The sound of the car's broken muffler shakes the early evening quiet. I can still hear the muffler's metal bounce and sputter as she pulls away from a stop sign two blocks away.

There's a group of kids walking and laughing across the street. Two of the boys play fight, trying to knock each other's backwards baseball caps off of each other's heads. I want to tell them to be easy on one another. How they're going to be fighting in this town for the rest of their lives. Save the energy. Take the time off when you can. I don't even have to look too close to see them. I don't even break stride really. Teeth already fucked up from their ValuTime sugar diets. The hand-me-down clothes. One boy wears a dirty white t-shirt that's two sizes too big for him with a logo for a whiskey company on the back. For a moment, I feel sorry for them. They're just children yelling for the attention they all need, that they're not getting anywhere else. When it comes down to it, they'll take anything they can get.

These thoughts get interrupted when I hear one of them yell the N-word at the other and all of my sympathy, the desire to do something to help them, circles down my emotional drain.

Just more poor angry white kids looking for someone to blame. I can't help them. Best I can do is help myself. The only person I've ever really been able to bring myself to blame.

"Ahh, Fuck 'em," I say out loud.

The church bells over at the United Methodist Church let me know that it's now 6:30 PM.

Chapter 75

I want to stop at the coffee shop before I leave but it's closed. I peer in through the front window. The lights are all off and I remember I never thought to get Marge's phone number, so I have no way of contacting her. I could use some kind of pep talk at the moment. Or just some of her energy. A conversation about life just being a game that we play and how it doesn't all have to be so serious all of the time.

"Henry!"

I turn my head and see Steve standing on the opposite corner.

"Hey Steve!"

Steve looks around, but there aren't any cars in sight. He jogs across the street and I meet him at the crosswalk.

"Henry, I heard a rumor about you. Is it true you're leaving?"

"It is. I'm actually heading to the grocery store right now to catch my bus."

"Just like that, huh? Do you have a place to stay and everything?"

"Yeah. I'm all set up. I just have to get there. I heard a rumor about you too."

"Shit. What did you hear?"

"That you're running for mayor? I'm assuming you're the *local bar owner with no political experience.*"

"Ha! You got me. Where'd you hear that?"

"An ad from the mayor on the radio. I figured it had to be you. Are you really going to run?"

"I don't know what I'm doing yet. The whole thing started out as a joke. No one has even run against him in the last two elections. I've never liked the guy and when I heard that it was going to happen again, I joked about it around the bar and everyone there was telling me I should. I was up late one night and got on the computer just to see what it takes to run. It turns out it's $35 bucks and 100 signatures. So, fuck it, I paid the $35 bucks and printed out the signature form. I brought it into the bar and hung it up next to the dart boards. I had the signatures I needed in two days. I don't know if they were all real or not, but like I said, it was all kind of a joke. So I took the papers up to City Hall and turned them in. The lady was shocked that anyone would even try to run against the guy. That pissed me off even more. Three days later, I get a phone call that I've been approved. And that's it. Thirty-five bucks and 100 people that don't hate you and you're in the race."

"I would think there would be a more to it."

"I'm sure there is in bigger places. But in a place like Brooksville, it's that easy. Anyway, two days after that I get a call from the Mayor. The actual Mayor is calling me at home and asking why I'm running against him. You could tell he was offended that anyone would even think to run against him. He asked me what I thought he was doing wrong and if I thought I could do any better. So I told him. There's nothing for the kids to do here. The drugs just keep coming and coming. And now he's trying to push that bill through that would stop the EMTs from having to save people when they OD. I mean, what kind of bullshit is that? You can't just let people die. That's the whole job! But he doesn't want to hear any of it, of course. And I'm just getting madder and madder about him calling me. The nerve of this guy! By the time the conversation was ending I was hot and I let him know. I told him he was in for the fight of his life."

"So you're really doing it? Mayor Steve?"

"Ha! I guess I am. If for no other reason than to piss that guy off."

"Are you gonna swing back after that ad? Or are you just gonna let him talk about you like that?"

"The way I figure it is no one under the age of 60 even listens to that station. He's got those votes already. I'm just gonna stick with the bar as my base. I'll start with my folks and move outward from there."

"So we're both making big moves."

"I guess so, Henry. I didn't mean to hold you up. I saw you from across the street and wanted to confirm the rumor. You need a shot before the bus ride? It's on me."

"I think I'm ok. I do need to get over there though. Good luck, Steve. I think you'd be good for this place."

"Thanks, Henry. And good luck to you. I'm happy for ya."

"Thanks Steve. Good luck with politics."

"Fucking politics," he says, shaking his head.

"To the death of the shoe salesman," I yell over my shoulder as we part ways.

Chapter 76

As I arrive at the grocery store, the United Methodist Church bells ring, letting me know that it's now 7 o'clock.

There's no bus station in Brooksville so the grocery-store parking lot is used for the bus drop-offs and pick-ups. I head into the store to buy a Coke and a copy of the *Lamplight* for the bus ride.

The automatic doors of the grocery store swoosh open and let me in. I grab a Coke from the cooler display on the end cap of the first checkout line, then a copy of the *Lamplight* from the rack at the register. I decide to try one of the self-checkout machines and get through without having to talk to anyone. I don't need a bag, but I grab one, figuring I can transfer a few things I might want for the ride from my backpack into the plastic grocery bag so they're easier to get to.

I'm on my way out when I see a cigarette advertisement over by the service counter. Somewhere in my brain, there is a small line that connects the idea of traveling and smoking. I decide I need cigarettes for the trip.

I buy two packs of Carolina Lights and a blue Bic lighter at the service desk. I take my backpack off and put one pack in the small front pocket of the backpack and put the other pack in the left front pocket of my jeans. I head outside to have a cigarette and think while I wait for my bus to arrive.

I walk out of the grocery store and find a bench around the corner next to a payphone. I think about the one in the front of the store; how people were always coming in and asking for their change back after they used it. Not so much anymore, with everyone having a cellphone now, but every once in a while. I set the grocery bag down on the bench and pick up the receiver. I put it to my ear and listen to the dial tone. I fish through my pockets and find two quarters. I plink them into the coin slot and punch Josh's number into the keypad. I let it ring twelve times before I finally hang up.

"Probably at work," I say to myself.

I scrape the two quarters out of the coin return with my middle finger and slide them back into my pocket. I move the grocery bag down on the bench, take my backpack off, and set it down next to it. I take a seat on the bench and just sit for a while. The whole world looks the same as always but I feel different. I don't know if I am different, but I feel different. The minutes slide by. I break down and pull out a pack of Carolina Lights.

There's something romantic about the ritual of smoking. I bang the top of the pack against my left palm, like I've seen my mother do a million times before. I'm not entirely sure what this does, but I figure I will learn soon enough. I unwrap the cellophane from the box and pull a cigarette free. I light up with my new Bic.

The first hit of the cigarette makes me cough. But after that it tastes smooth. I take big deep drag and blow the smoke out slowly. After the first couple of drags, my mind starts to wobble. It feels like it's encased in liquid. I think about calling my mom to see if she's home. Maybe she'd calmed down and would come up and see her son off to his new life. I liked that thought and I kicked it around for a few minutes before abandoning it. I know it will be better if I wait until I get to Josh's to call her. Give her a little more time to absorb the idea of me being gone.

I take another lung full of smoke and try unsuccessfully to blow a smoke ring into the air. And then another. I think about my sister Kaitlyn and how I never got to know her. I wonder where Rick is right now and what he's doing. Something is missing in my goodbye. It's incomplete. The idea of calling my mom returns. I stand up and put those two same quarters back into the coin slot of the payphone. I have to concentrate to dial the number. The call goes through, but as soon as I hear it start to ring, I get scared and hang up.

I drop the cigarette onto the pavement and smash it into the ground. I immediately feel bad for doing so, knowing some poor person like myself will be out here tonight with a broom chasing these things down. I reach down and pick the butt back up. I find a garbage can around the corner and toss it in.

I'm walking back to my bench, still light-headed, when I turn the corner and bump into someone.

"I'm so sorry. I wasn't watching where I was going." I apologize.

"Well, well, look who it is."

"Marge!"

I can't believe it's her. My head is still swimming with the nicotine buzz, but seeing Marge calms me. She is what's missing.

"What are you doing here?" I ask.

"I came to buy groceries, but it looks like maybe I'm here for another reason now. You're all packed up, I see."

"I am. The bus leaves at 8. I can't believe you're here! I just tried calling my mom, but I got freaked out when it started to ring. I think I'm scared. Or maybe terrified is a better word."

"Good. You should be. I'd be more worried if you weren't. It's a big world, Henry. But you don't have to be afraid. Millions of people have done this before. It's a big step, but a very important one in finding out who you really are .... I didn't know you smoked."

I look down at my hands like they aren't mine. Out of nervousness I have pulled the pack out of my pocket and started digging around for another cigarette.

"I don't. I thought it was a romantic thing to do for some reason."

"It is, but there's no reason. Just throw them away when you get to where you're going. Trust me."

"I will. It just seemed like what a character would do in a movie if they were getting ready for a bus trip. It's dumb, I know."

"It's ok. Don't be so hard on yourself."

"Do you have everything you need? Is that all that you're taking? Those two little bags?" Marge waves a silver and turquoise-ringed hand in the direction of the bench.

"I don't need much. I figure I can buy clothes and anything else I might need after I find a job. I didn't want to be traveling with a bunch of stuff. And I honestly, I didn't have much more than what I have with me."

"Traveling light," Marge says and gives me a wink. "Smart."

I can't believe she has shown up here at this very moment. My brain is searching for a proper thank you when I see the bus pulling off the side street and into the grocery-store parking lot. It's big and intimidating with its blacked-out windows and loud diesel engine. We watch as the bus winds slowly and carefully through the rows of parked cars. The brakes squeal as it pulls up in front of the bench my bags are sitting on. There's a loud hiss when it stops, and the whole vehicle seems to sink just a little from the pressure being released.

"Well, looks like it's time for you to go, Henry."

"I guess so."

Marge reaches out and wraps her arms around me. I think about how I've been hugged more today than I have since I was a child. If nothing else, the trip has been worth that.

"It's time to go," Marge says softly, striking a soothing motherly tone.

Her voice makes the world seem much more calm. My anxiety level ticks down a notch and makes the situation suddenly seem manageable.
Some people just have a way with the world. The rest of us need to remember to listen.

"Thank you," I say."For everything. I can never repay you for this. For your friendship. For everything."

"You get on that bus and you can consider us even."

Marge reaches into her purse and rummages around. She pulls out her wallet and opens it up. She pulls a one-hundred dollar bill from a larger stack of bills, reaches out, and grabs my hand. She places the money in my palm and wraps my fingers into a fist around the bill.

"I'm not sure what your situation is when you get there, but a little money always helps."

I feel a tear run down my face as I open my mouth to tell her I can't accept the money. That she has already done so much for me. But she waves it all of my words away. She keeps her left hand wrapped around my right fist.

"Just hold onto it for me," she says with a wink.

There was nothing more I could say to her. The dam burst and I felt my shoulders heave. I reached out and hugged her with all of the emotion left inside of me.

"Thank you, Marge. For everything."

"It's my pleasure, Henry. I've gotten more from this friendship than I have given. It's the least I can do."

We continue to embrace for a moment then break apart. Marge's eyes are so kind and in that moment I wish I could see myself the way she sees me.

"You don't want to miss your bus now," she says. "Let me give you my number, though. If you need anything, anything at all, you just call me, ok?"

"I will. I promise."

She pulls a pen from her purse and searches for a piece of paper. She finds a receipt and writes her phone number down on the back side. She hands it to me and tells me again to call if I need anything.
I put it in my pocket and hug her quickly one last time.

The hiss of the hydraulic doors of the bus finally opening startles the both of us. We both take a step away from one another and I wipe my eyes with the sleeve of my jacket.

"Don't forget your bags," Marge tells me.

"I won't. Don't forget the milk."

We wave to one another one last time as she walks off and into the grocery store.

Chapter 77

I pick up my backpack and walk over to the bus doors. I climb up the stairs and the old man behind the wheel smiles, but doesn't say anything as I hand him my ticket. I walk down the aisle scanning the rows for a seat. There are only four people on the entire bus and there doesn't seem to be anyone else getting on at this stop. In the very last seat on the right side there's a woman holding a baby and they're both looking out the window while she bounces the child up and down on her lap.

I walk straight back and take the first seat in the aisle across from them. She looks up as I make my way toward the back and smiles, probably hoping that I won't sit near her, but I do. I take my backpack off and place it underneath the seat. I set the plastic grocery bag on the seat next to me.

We wait in the parking lot for another few minutes. The driver sits at the wheel reading a book about Spain while listening to a spring training baseball game being played down in Florida. I can hear the announcer's familiar voice. He announces the games that are broadcast during the summer on WQRC.

I double check my pockets for my wallet, cigarettes, and the money that Marge gave me. Everything is where it's supposed to be.

The church bells ring. It's eight o'clock.

The driver jerks his head up from his book and looks into the back of the bus through the rearview mirror. He gives a glance outside to make sure no one is trying to catch the bus last minute. After looking around the parking lot, he reaches for the lever on his right and yanks on it, pulling the doors closed. My heart is jerks to attention and lodges itself inside of my throat.

The idling engine suddenly comes alive. I feel its rumble in my bones all the way in the backseat.

The driver rolls the bus slowly through the parking lot, making the turn to aim us west. I can barely contain my excitement. I smile and look around to see if everyone else feels it too. The other four adults on the bus look bored and uninterested. I glance over to the lady and her baby and see that the baby is now sound asleep on her shoulder.

We drive two blocks west before making the big left turn onto Main Street. The driver points us south and we make our way slowly through downtown. I sit and watch as we pass the coffee shop and then the jewelry store. I think of Josh telling me that the fall from the rooftop wasn't enough to kill me.

We make our way to the south end and I see Mel standing outside the store smoking as we pass. I wave out of excitement and reflex before quickly realizing it's impossible for her to see me through the blackout windows. I crane my neck to watch her for as long as

I can. I watch her flick her cigarette butt towards the gas pumps and head back inside.

We come to the end of town and pull out onto the county road, heading southwest. The businesses and houses end and we begin cutting into the corn and soybean fields of the county. About eight miles out, we cross into a new county and I remind myself that from here on out everything is brand new. We drive on this county road for 17 miles before we come upon another small town. This is where the county road connects with an actual state highway. The driver pulls into a small gas station and pulls up to the only diesel pump on the far end of the property.

"Ten minutes," he yells back to us.

The few people up front gather themselves and stand up. I'm not sure what to do so I sit and watch before making a move. Two of the folks up front walk off the bus and go into the gas station. I figure it's safe as long as I'm not the last one back on. I stand up and slide towards the aisle. The lady on the other side of the aisle looks up and we make eye contact for a split second before she quickly turns away. The baby is still asleep on her shoulder.

I climb off the bus and walk over in the direction of a trashcan that sits next to the big white ice cooler. I reach for my cigarettes and pull one out. I light it up and take a deep pull of smoke. I notice the nicotine calm as it hits me and am thankful for my short-term habit. A few minutes slide by as I enjoy the cigarette. When I'm done, I snuff it out on the trashcan lid then drop the butt inside. I climb back on the bus and make my way back to my seat. The other passengers get back on shortly after me and the driver follows them in. He takes a headcount and decides we're ready to leave.

We pull out onto the county road and make a right turn onto the state highway. The speed limit jumps up to sixty-five and you can feel the speed as the bus begins a gentle rock and sway. My body and brain lock in on the engine's soothing hum.

The first sign I see out the window says we're 185 miles away from the city. I had never traveled so far in my entire life.

I feel the bus driver shift gears.

The fast-food chains and Walmarts appear and disappear as we make our way through all of the small towns of the state. I feel myself calming down and settling in. I reach over and pull the latest issue of *Memory Currency* out of the plastic grocery bag on the seat next to me.

I haven't made it through the entire issue yet and my newly imagined theory has reignited my interest in the series.I open it up to where I left off and started reading. I find Captain Jane with her blue hair living under water.

From there it skips around to different character, a fish wearing a dunce cap.

Even with my newfound excitement for the book, the entire thing feels off the rails. I re-read the first six pages three times. I'm about to give up on the entire issue when I mindlessly flip to page 16.

Here's Captain Jane drawn dead and bleeding from her red-haired head. Her face is mangled and there's a gun lying just out of reach of her right hand. My heart sinks.

If my theory is correct, this represents the author either wanting to kill himself or maybe just the idea of death.

There is no dialogue or word bubbles on the page. I flip to the next page and find that it's blank.

I frantically turn the remaining pages, only to find them all blank. I reach the last two pages and find these words written in bold black ink on the plain white paper:

I AM SORRY.

THE END.

I don't know what to think. Has the author killed himself? Has he just killed the character? Was he just out of ideas?

I have no revelations. No new theories. I feel betrayed and a little sick hoping that the author is somewhere writing something new and not dead.

The bus continues to rock and sway as I flip back and forth through the pages. I realize I'm too worked up over a comic book when the thought that I need a cigarette jumps into my brain.I set *Memory Currency* down on the empty seat next to me and focus my attention back out the window.

I put my cheek against the cool glass and take deep breaths. I think about arriving at the bus station and how excited Josh will be to see me and how excited I am to see him. How I don't have to go to work tonight. And in the morning I don't have to walk back home to sleep in an empty apartment. I relax and reach into the grocery bag and pull out the stack of letters from Josh.

I take the rubber band off and run my fingers through them like a deck of cards. I glance out the window and catch a sign that says we are only 100 miles out of the city.

I pull a letter from the bottom of the stack and set the others aside on the seat next to me, next to the copy of *Memory Currency*.

I pull the letter out of the envelope and start to read.

Dear Henry,

I'm sorry I had to leave without you. I got the opportunity and I had to take it. I'll get things started here and you can come down as soon as you're ready.

Your friend,

Josh

I smile and think back to the day that I got this first letter and how upset I was that he had left without me. How long ago that had been and of everything that had happened in between. It seemed ludicrous now that it had taken me so long. I pick the envelope up to see the date that it was sent, but I find that there's no stamp or date. Just my name and my address on the front of the envelope. I pull another letter from the stack.

Henry,

Any plans on coming down to visit? I'd love to see you, but I don't think I'll be able to get back to town anytime soon. Work has me pretty busy and I don't think I can start taking any time off yet. Let me know.

Josh

I check the envelope for this letter for an address and date, but again there's no stamp or date. Just my name addressed on the front.

My hands are sweating and the letter feels damp in my hand. I look out the window and see the cornfields and billboards for lawyers going by. I can feel my heart beating in my throat.

I pick another letter at random from the stack and pull it from the envelope.

Henry,

I'm sorry I left but you seem like you're doing ok? Are you doing ok? Am I ok? And what is going on with Memory Currency? Is there more to it? I think there's something about Captain Jane. A connection to your grandfather maybe?

I'm sorry I had to leave. I'm not sure when or if I'll be back.

Your friend,
Josh

I don't remember ever getting this letter. And it doesn't seem to make any sense.

I feel sweat starting to drip under my arms. My face feels hot and I can't seem to catch my breath.

I reach for another letter. My hands are shaking.

I accidentally fumble and the entire stack spills down onto the floor of the bus. My mouth is starting to water and I feel like I could throw up. I look around to see if there's a bathroom on the bus, but my eyes start to blur. I get down on my knees and onto the floor and start frantically trying to scoop the letters up, but they've scattered all over the floor of the bus.

I grasp desperately for the letters and manage to get a bunch in my hands and dump them back onto the seat next to me. I grab one at random. No stamp. No date. Just my name. I grab another. No stamp. No date. I can feel the tears starting to run down my face and my voice quietly starting to say *No* while moving up in pitch.

I open another letter:

Henry, What the fuck is wrong with you? What are you doing? You are exactly like your grandfather. It would be best if you stay as far away from people as possible. You can only cause pain. It's all that you know.

I see Rick's face exploding with blood. I can feel the bottle in my hands. The heat in my lungs when I was running away. The knife against my throat and how did Rick know where I lived? And him telling me to stay away from the tequila. I hear my mom telling me not to leave town. My grandfather wandering off for weeks. My empty apartment.

I hear the sound of my own voice again, rising even higher in pitch. I have no idea what I'm saying. I'm watching myself from above.

I fall to the floor of the bus searching for other letters. I see an envelope two rows up and I scramble on my knees towards it. I hear the baby beside me starting to cry and the mother is asking me if I'm ok. Her voice is soft, but also shaky and scared.

"I'm fine! I'm fine!" I blurt out, before lowering my voice. "I just dropped something. I'm ok. I promise."

I open the letter I've picked up from the floor and try to read it, but I can't make out any of the words.

I feel the bus brake and I go tumbling forward. I get back to my knees, but as soon as I do, I throw up into the aisle.

I hear the child crying.

I hear the mother yelling for the driver to stop.

I feel the swerve of the bus as I reach for a seat next to me to steady myself.

I hear Rick's voice in my head and I see my little sister Kaitlyn dying in my arms.

I see Gina's unborn baby in the toilet of the gas station and my mother telling me we might both have been better off if she never had me in the first place.

I feel the knife against my throat and hear Rick's thick, drunk voice calling me son.

I hear that sunny voice on the radio that I despise.

"WQRC: The Hits You Miss!!! Here's the Chordettes with their 1958 hit!!! Lollipop, Lollipop, oh, lolli, lollipop, POP! Have we got some birthdays today!!!"

I reach for the pack of cigarettes in my pocket and light one up while sitting on the floor of the bus.

The bus has come to a stop and I hear the driver telling me I can't smoke and then asking if I'm ok.

I hear the other passengers talking in hushed concern voices. If the baby in the back would just stop crying, I think I could think straight but I'm not sure.

"Can you please shut that baby the fuck up!"

I think that is my voice. But I know that can't be my voice. I would never say anything like that.

I crawl through my own vomit back to my seat.

I reach into my backpack and find a pen in the small front pocket.

I press one of the letters down onto the hard plastic seat and steady my hand.

If that baby would just stop crying...

I write my name: *Henry*.

And the words: *You almost made it*.

The handwriting is identical to the handwriting in all of the letters.

I look up and see the lady next to me holding her baby close to her chest. She is terrified. I want to tell her that it's all ok. And that I'm ok. That we'll all be ok, but I know that's not true.

The easiest thing in this world is to become the very thing you fear the most.

ACKNOWLEDGEMENTS:

Thank you to the people of Brooksville for allowing me to view your lives inside of my head for two years. To Vanessa Jean Speckman for creating the artwork for the book and bringing Brooksville to life. Paulette Poullet for helping us piece all of these visuals together. And finally, thank you to Michael Baron and White Gorilla Press for believing in me and having the patience to help me see this whole thing through.

Micah Schnabel is a songwriter/writer from Bucyrus, Ohio. He is a founding member of the band Two Cow Garage and a prolific solo artist. He currently resides in Columbus, Ohio. This is his first novel. You can find him on tour in a town near you.

You can find more of his work at
micahschnabel.bandcamp.com

Vanessa Jean Speckman is a visual and textual artist from Saratoga, California.

You can view more of her work at
www.etsy.com/shop/VanessaJeanSpeckman